HIGHLAND TREASURE

Highland Heartstrings, Book 1

by

Brenna Ash

ARE YOU SIGNED UP FOR DRAGONBLADE'S BLOG?

You'll get the latest news and information on exclusive giveaways, exclusive excerpts, coming releases, sales, free books, cover reveals and more.

Check out our complete list of authors, too!

No spam, no junk. That's a promise!

Sign Up Here

www.dragonbladepublishing.com

Dearest Reader;

Thank you for your support of a small press. At Dragonblade Publishing, we strive to bring you the highest quality Historical Romance from some of the best authors in the business. Without your support, there is no 'us', so we sincerely hope you adore these stories and find some new favorite authors along the way.

Happy Reading!

CEO, Dragonblade Publishing

Additional Dragonblade books by Author Brenna Ash

Highland Heartstrings Series
Highland Treasure (Book 1)

Rogues of Redemption Series
Sweet Rogue O' Mine (Book 1)
Rogue You Like a Hurricane (Book 2)
No Rogue Like You (Book 3)
Nobody's Rogue (Book 4)
Here I Rogue Again (Book 5)

The Lyon's Den Series
The Lyon's Last Gamble

CHAPTER ONE

Scottish Highlands
Spring, 1394

MOIRA HART ROLLED her eyes as she descended the stairs that would take her deep into the bowels of Hartsmoor Castle. She'd left her two older brothers arguing over the last currant tart available from Una's most recent batch. There was no doubt their cook's tarts were indeed worth fighting over, but Moira had heard and seen enough when the two dolts looked like they were going to break into fisticuffs over who would get to partake in the remaining sweet.

If they'd use their too stubborn heads for a moment, they'd realize cutting the tart in half would allow them to each enjoy the treat. But, alas, that was too much to ask of them, so she left them to battle it out in the way they always did.

She paused on the steps, took a deep breath of the somewhat stagnant air, and listened.

There was not a sound to be heard down here, and she reveled in the quietness. These times of solitude were her favorite and she enjoyed them immensely. She adored her family, but sometimes her parents and her four siblings could be a wee bit overwhelming. Continuing her descent, she reached the bottom and turned left, entering the narrow tunnel that would lead her even deeper underground and to the place she loved to spend all her time—the Hart clan archives.

"""

Late last year, Moira's father, Arthur Hart, laird of the northern Hart clan, had tasked her with putting the family annals in order. The room had long been neglected. Tomes, scrolls, ledgers, and parchments were stacked haphazardly all around the enclosed space. Overflowing shelves bowed under the weight of the artifacts they held. So much so, that Moira feared they would break in two and collapse if she didn't provide order soon. Luckily, the stone-walled room was dry and safe from outside elements, so other than piles of dust, all of the items remained intact and undamaged.

The written history dated back hundreds of years—back when the Harts came to Scotland from Ireland—and she felt like it would take her that long to put the room in order.

Hands on her hips, Moira looked around, turning in a slow circle, trying to assess the best way to tackle the monumental task.

She had no complaints, though. Fascinated by history, putting order to all of her family's most important artifacts was a deed she took seriously. Her brothers and sisters just shook their heads, not understanding her interest in 'old, boring parchments'.

Their reactions didn't sway her in any way. She couldn't wait to dive in and learn all the big and little details that made the Harts the strong clan that they were today.

Nestled in the highlands, they were a small, but mighty clan. Not the smallest, but certainly not the largest. Her father led their people with confidence, keeping the peace with neighboring clans as best he could—with the exception of the MacLeod.

It seemed that no matter what they tried, or what truces the Harts offered, the MacLeods were determined to continue the unrest betwixt them. At times, they had enjoyed small stretches of peace, but there was always something that would happen to end the fragile agreements.

Moira could remember a time when her older brothers, Alpin and Rory, had enjoyed good friendships with the MacLeod sons. Ofttimes, they would traipse through the woods together, hunt together, even sword practice together. But, for whatever reason, that ceased years ago. Now she only saw Errol, one of the MacLeod sons, from a distance when he would visit with his father during tenuous meetings, where more growling than talking was done. And where Alpin and Rory would only exchange scowls with Errol, fists balled at their sides. When the meeting would end, with naught being solved, both leaders would part gruffly, and things would continue the same way as they had been.

Errol, firstborn son of the MacLeod clan, was tall, the same height as her brother Rory, but while Rory was lean and lithe, Errol was bulging with muscles. Massively broad shoulders gave him a wide expanse and his arms were big as logs. He was built much like her brother Alpin.

And he was handsome. Though she would never admit that. Not aloud anyway.

She could only shake her head. Men made things overly difficult. How hard was it to talk to one another?

A chill hung in the air and the torch that Moira had carried down with her and placed in the sconce didn't help to warm the space. For not the first time since she'd started coming down here, she wished there was a fireplace in this room. It made sense that there wasn't. The absence of flame eliminated the possibility that the contents of the room would be lost to fire.

Such an event would be devastating. All this history lost. To ensure that prevention, she would happily suffer the cool air. That's what her heavy cloak was for. Pulling the strings at her neck tighter, Moira tied them into a bow and got to work.

Quite some time had passed when footsteps sounded in the tunnel outside of the room. Moments later, her younger sister, Eilidh, poked her head inside, scrunching her nose in disgust as she looked around the room.

"Of course, ye are here," she announced, twirling her long hair around her slim fingers. "Mama was looking for ye."

Moira straightened, her arms filled with stacks of parchments. "Why?"

"I didnae ask." Eilidh shrugged. "Though why she thought ye would be anywhere else but here, I dinnae ken."

"Weel, it cannae have been verra important if she didnae tell ye what she needs me for." She looked around the room and set the stack of papers on a large table one of the guards had dragged in from the storage room next door at her request. "I'm almost done here for the day." She rubbed her hands together to get some warmth back into her fingertips.

Eilidh shuddered from the cold. "How ye can spend yer days down here baffles me." She rubbed her hands up and down her arms. "'Tis no' only cold, but creepy," she said as she looked around the room.

Moira laughed. "Nonsense. Go back upstairs and tell mama that I will be there shortly. I just have a few more things I want to set to order first."

Alone once again, she finished clearing off the shelf stack that was against one of the walls. Her plan was to move it to the opposite side of the room because the table would fit better in this space. When it was empty, she attempted to pull the shelving away from the wall. Grunting with exertion, she tugged harder. The piece was heavy. Much heavier than she originally thought it would be.

She managed to get it away from the wall a wee smidge, with just enough space for her to wiggle her fingers into. That gave her a slight advantage and allowed her to maneuver it a little further away from the wall.

Perspiration pooled at the small of her back. The room may be chilly, but just the amount of energy it was taking to move the shelving was a lot. If she wasn't so stubborn, she would have gone upstairs and asked for the help of one of her brothers. Or a guard. But she didn't want to run into her mother since she was already looking for Moira and more than likely she would forbid her from returning here this eve.

Determination had her furrowing her brow as she alternately pushed and pulled at the shelving unit until finally, she could squeeze her body between the wooden frame and the stone wall. Using her body weight, slight as it was, she managed to push the shelving a couple of feet away from the wall, allowing her to get all the way behind the shelves.

Sliding against the wall, her plan was to use the wall to brace her back and hands against it while she used her feet to push the shelving further away. Gently, though. She didn't want to topple it over. If that happened, she would never be able to lift it up and set it to rights. However, as she slid, using her hands to guide her, her fingers slid over wood.

Brows creased, Moira backed out of the space and tried to see what she had touched. It was too dark to see anything. She grabbed the torch from the wall and careful, so as not to touch any of the items and set them ablaze, she shone the light in the space.

With a gasp, she saw a small door. With a simple handle and black iron hinges, it measured mayhap two feet tall and a foot wide.

Whyever would there be a door hidden behind the shelves, she wondered. For her answer she would need to create more space.

And get a lantern. It would be much safer in the small area.

Did she dare risk going upstairs to grab one? Surely her mother would see her. She'd be on the lookout for Moira since undoubtedly Eilidh told her where she was.

Lillias Hart, their mother, would never venture down here. She didn't like the space and continuously warned Moira about spending too much time in the cold, dark tunnel and room. Her mother worried that she would catch her death.

It was all silly, really. It was colder outside than here, but her mother always said at least outside, the air was fresh. It wasn't the stagnant, stale air of centuries that was trapped in the rooms below, harboring unknown diseases.

Crossing her arms, she thrummed her fingers against her upper arm.

"What to do, what to do?" she asked the empty room.

She went out into the tunnel and the steps to the upper floors, but instead of climbing them, she turned to her left and walked down the long corridor. There were more storerooms on this side, along with the dungeon, which she steered clear from, even though no one was being held there. Nobody had for a very long time.

In one of the storage rooms, she found an unlit lantern and snatched it to bring back to the archive room.

Dragging a small table from the corner, Moira set it against the wall near the shelving unit and lit it. The dark space behind the shelves lit up in a warm glow, the lantern's reflection dancing off the iron hinges of the door.

It looked ancient. The wood worn smooth with time.

Moira settled herself back into the space, sliding along the wall until the door was right in front of her. There was no lock. Just a simple hook and latch that she released with a creak. The place was too cramped to open the door fully, so bracing her hands on the wall, she pushed her bottom out against the shelving, trying to budge it away and open the space up more. The unit scraped along the stone floor, echoing off the stone walls. The loud noise pierced her ears and made Moira's head want to split.

Finally, she'd created enough space to allow her to open the door fully. She studied it for a moment, and glanced toward the hall, listening to hear if anyone was about.

It almost felt as if she was doing something forbidden.

What would she find? If anything.

She pulled on the handle, but it didn't budge. The door seemed to be jammed. After coming this far, Moira wasn't about to let it go. She shimmied the handle to and fro, trying to loosen it. When the door moved just a bit, she smiled. Her progress was slow, but it was working.

Concentrating, she kept working at it and, after what seemed forever, she could finally open the door fully. When she did, she held her breath as she peered inside the small space. The stone had been carved out, making a small alcove that someone had covered with the door.

Interesting.

There was only one thing inside—a small scroll.

Moira plucked it out and blew off the layer of dust that had built up over time and waved her hands through the air to clear it. She pulled on the brittle string holding it closed, the fragile material fell apart as she tugged. Whatever this was, it was old.

Ancient even.

Biting her lip, she unfurled the parchment, the edges were cracked and yellowed with age, and her breath caught at what was revealed.

In her hands she held a map. But not just any map.

It was a map that hinted to a long-lost treasure.

A Hart family treasure.

Studying the old script and drawing, her eyes rounded.

MacLeod lands were listed as well. Had the MacLeods claimed land from the Harts? She had no idea, but she would need to find out.

Her pulse quickened with excitement. A treasure hunt sounded fun.

The only problem was she would need to get onto MacLeod lands. She frowned. How could she manage that?

Then it came to her.

She would need to enlist Errol MacLeod's help.

It wouldn't be easy. He was just as stubborn as her brothers.

The realization that she would need his assistance had her pulse quickening. From fear or excitement, she wasn't sure.

But she would find out soon.

$$\longleftrightarrow$$

CHAPTER TWO

THE CLANG OF metal crashing together echoed in the air as men practiced their fighting skills in the yard. Errol MacLeod felt the force of the strike he'd just blocked reverberate down his arm.

He smiled. "Yer skill is improving, Angus," he commended his young cousin, and the lad grinned broadly.

"I've the best tutor."

At the age of ten and three, Angus was tall and well on his way to growing as big, if not bigger, than his father—Errol's uncle.

"Go wash up. Ye did well today."

Errol scanned the courtyard. His father's men had been training hard all day. An exercise that was important to ensure the safety of their clan. Thankfully, they hadn't needed to fight in recent months, though the harsh weather of winter was to thank for that. However, it was a nice break from the constant raids and battles of the past.

"Care for a spar?"

Errol turned to see his cousin Robbie waiting for him to accept the challenge. Being the same age, he and Robbie had grown up together and were close as brothers.

"I see ye had yer hands full with Angus," he jested.

"Dinnae pick on yer brother. He works hard to prove himself."

Robbie tapped him on the shoulder with the tip of his sword. Errol brought his own sword up and used it to put distance between the two of them.

The men circled each other.

"He'll make a fine warrior one day." Errol said as Robbie lunged forward and he stepped to the side, swinging back around and catching his cousin on the upper left arm, careful to hit with the flat side of his blade.

"Lucky shot," Robbie huffed.

Errol shrugged. "Angus is going to be of formidable size once he's fully grown."

Robbie beamed with pride, as if the lad was his own.

"Aye." Robbie swung and Errol brought his sword up to defend the strike.

His cousin was strong, but he was stronger. Back and forth they went, until they were both spent and breathing hard.

A messenger entered, and Errol called him over. The young boy wore the colors of the Harts and Errol's eyes narrowed. What the hell did they want now? The two clans had shared a tumultuous past. They weren't in an outright war, but they also wouldn't hesitate to attack if they felt one of them had been wronged in any way.

Beside him, Robbie crossed his arms and pierced the lad with a stern look.

"I bring a message for Miss Anna from Miss Moira."

He should have guessed as much. Laird Hart wouldn't send a lad to deliver a message of official business.

Errol sighed. No matter how much strife continued betwixt the two clans, his sister and the eldest Hart daughter would not cease their friendship. He motioned to the keep.

"Go to the kitchens and get yerself a meal for yer work." He held out his hand and the lad gave the message to him. He'd bring it to Anna.

There was no need to read it first. He'd made that mistake in the past. He had no interest in the menial conversations of lasses, especially ones betwixt his younger sister and her friend.

"They are still communicating?" Robbie asked. "I am surprised yer da hasnae put an end to it."

Errol shook his head. "'Tis no' for his lack of trying. Anna is as stubborn as he is."

Robbie chuckled. "A family trait, I'd say."

With a scowl, Errol shouldered past his cousin in search of his sister.

He found her speaking to her maid, Fina, in the hall leading to the kitchens. He should have just had the messenger deliver the damn note since they were in the same area.

Anna scrunched her nose as he approached.

"Brother, ye should clean up afore entering the kitchens. Maighread will have yer head if she sees ye." She waved her hand in front of her face. "Though likely she'll smell ye before she sees ye."

His sister and her maid giggled.

He cocked his head to the side and fought the urge to roll his eyes. Instead, he held his hand out. "A message from Moira has arrived for ye."

Anna snatched the missive from his hand and cradled it to her chest, then eyed him suspiciously, her eyes narrowed. "Did ye read it?" she asked.

"Nay. I've better ways to spend my time." Errol turned on his heel and left the girls giggling after him.

He wondered if he could convince his father into arranging another trip to Hart lands to meet with Laird Hart and his council. The meeting would result in naught, however, mayhap Errol would be able to catch a glimpse or two of bonny Moira. He'd seen her the past few times they'd met, and his body roared to life each time.

Errol remembered her from when he and her brothers actually ly spent time as friends instead of enemies when they were younger. She used to trail behind them trying to keep up. Not any longer, though.

Now she was grown with pale blue eyes, shaped like a cat's, and fringed with long lashes. Her dark blonde hair fell in thick waves over her shoulders. Her skin was the color of ivory and he could only imagine that it would be soft as velvet under his fingertips.

Clearing his throat, he discreetly adjusted himself as he continued to his bedchamber to wash up. His body didn't care that they could never be together. The animosity between their two clans would never allow it.

But in his mind, his thoughts ran rampant.

When he thought of the Hart brothers, anger had him clenching his fists. They were so smug during every meet. So much so that Errol wanted to march up to them and beat the smirks off their faces. They wouldn't be so assured then. Like Alpin, the eldest Hart sibling, Errol would also one day be laird.

The strife between them and their clans would continue even then. He could sense it. Jaw clenched, he stomped up the stairs.

They'd been fighting off and on for so many years that both lairds would be hard pressed to say what exactly was the cause of the strife. Their clans were similar in size, though the MacLeod was slightly larger. With the Hart owning slightly larger lands.

Errol only kenned he hated them.

The Harts could not be trusted.

Even if they had shared brief respites of fighting in past years, it was never enough for them to solve their grievances. Whatever grievances those might be.

He also believed they had other worries. Bigger clans from the north that would attack if they got the chance. Smaller clans from the west that, whilst they wouldn't attempt a full-on attack on their own, they'd had no qualms sending out small parties to steal sheep and cattle, or to hunt on MacLeod lands.

In his chamber, he splashed cool water on his face before pulling his tunic over his head. He ran the cloth he'd soaked with water across his chest, wiping away the sweat and dirt from his sword practice earlier.

Stripping off his trews, he washed below his waist, his cock heavy in his hands at the thoughts of Moira running rampant through his mind once again.

"Fool," he mumbled in the empty room, angry with himself for thinking of the enemy with anything other than hatred.

After drying off, he dressed in a clean tunic and trews and made his way back to the kitchens.

Maighread, the MacLeod cook, smiled as he entered and waved him into a chair. Within moments, she'd set a tankard of ale and a plate of crusty bread, cheese, and dried meats in front of him. "Eat. Are ye losing weight? Ye look like it."

He wasn't. It was just her way to mother him. Something she had done since he'd lost his mother years ago when she was birthing Anna.

Clearing the plate, he thanked the cook and left in search of his father.

"Brother."

He paused at Anna's call and spun around. The look she had on her face told him that he wouldn't like what she was going to say. Being the youngest MacLeod sibling and one that had never had the chance to know their beautiful mother, all the MacLeod men held a soft spot in their hearts for her.

Even Errol, whose heart had long been hardened, had a difficult time refusing his little sister whatever she asked for.

She held her hand up, waving the letter the messenger had delivered.

He frowned. It was because of her circumstances that they even allowed the friendship between she and Moira to continue. They'd met during one of the times of peace and both refused to give up on the other.

"What do ye require?" He asked.

Anna shook her head. "Naught. I only need to speak to ye."

Errol crossed his arms and looked down at his sister, eyebrows raised in question. "Go on, then."

She looked around the corridor they were standing in.

"No' here." Grabbing his hand, she pulled him toward one of the small antechambers they saved for guests. Once inside, Anna closed the door behind them.

"Are ye daft?"

His sister pierced him with an annoyed look. "As ye ken, I received a letter from Moira."

He kept his face neutral, refusing to let anyone ken the effect the lass had on him. "As ye have had many times afore."

"Right. But this time she is asking for help."

"Help how?" He couldn't keep the interest out of his voice.

"I am no' sure, exactly. She didnae say. Only that she needs to enlist yer assistance."

Errol scoffed. "She has her brothers to ask help of."

"Aye, she does. Though it sounds like this is something that she doesnae want to make them aware of."

He moved to take the note out of Anna's hand, but she snapped her hand back. "She doesnae speak of specifics. Only that she needs ye. Specifically, ye," she reiterated.

Looking over her shoulder, he glared at the wall and clenched his jaw. It could be a trap. Had someone learned of his admiration of the lass? In doing so, were they now trying to use that against him? It was the oldest trick to try to lure a man in with the promise of a beautiful lass.

He wouldn't be one to fall for it.

"I cannae help her. If, indeed, that is what she is asking."

It was Anna's turn to cross her arms. "Why no'?"

"Ye verra weel ken why. Da and I have allowed ye two to continue yer friendship e'en though it goes against e'erything we believe. Ye two are innocent in the conflict. Howe'er, dinnae push us on this. Whate'er she needs, she can discuss with her brothers and father."

"Ye are so stubborn. Why can ye no' help?" She shook the paper in the air. "She wrote asking for ye for a reason. There has to be a reason she isnae involving her siblings."

Errol sighed, pushing his hands through his hair.

"I cannae. 'Tis too dangerous. There are things ye dinnae need to fash yerself o'er. Ye should consider yerself lucky that ye neednae think of such things. Now, go find Fina and dinnae speak of this again."

"But—"

He felt bad denying Anna her request, but this was one he couldn't, wouldn't budge on.

"Nay. Enough."

Not wanting to entertain his sister's antics any longer, he left her and made his way to the stables. He had a new horse that he was in the process of training. The beast huffed when he entered, bobbing his black head up and down in greeting. Errol offered him a carrot from the bushel beside the stalls and the horse happily accepted the treat.

He ran his hands slowly down the horse's mane, speaking in low tones. "Ye'll make a fine warhorse one day, Dubh Bàn." The name meant black and white, and he fit the moniker perfectly since whilst he was mostly black, he had a perfect white circle on his right rear flank. As if the horse understood his words, he dipped his head and bumped Errol's shoulder.

Leading him out to the corral, he walked the horse in a wide circle, giving him time to adjust to the feel of having the saddle on him. Errol hadn't ridden him yet. No one had. The beast was a little too wild for the others and most gave him a wide berth so as not to draw his ire and a kick.

As Dubh Bàn continued trotting in circles, Errol's mind wandered. To places it shouldn't. To people it shouldn't. To a certain lass in particular that it shouldn't.

It made no sense that Moira was asking specifically for him. He could offer her naught on top of what her brothers could. But Anna was insistent. And why wouldn't Moira tell Anna what it was she needed him for and why?

Again, it had to be a trap. Something her brothers and father had conceived.

Right?

He swore. Irritated that he'd allowed Moira to get under his skin.

CHAPTER THREE

Moira frowned as she read the missive from Anna. Why were men so stubborn? She needed Errol's help. In her response, Anna said that her brother suggested enlisting her own brothers for any help she needed. Considering the map pointed her to MacLeod lands, her brothers would be of no assistance whatsoever. They would outright refuse at the mention of their rival clan. She and Anna got along just fine. She didn't understand how men couldn't do the same.

Somehow, some way, she needed to convince Errol MacLeod to help her in her quest. Mayhap if she offered him part of the treasure the map promised. That might do it.

It had been four days since she'd found the hidden door and the map. Luckily, her family stayed away from the annals room. For certs, they would question her about it if they saw it, and demand she ignored it.

She preferred to keep it her own secret for now.

The prospect of adventure made her heart beat faster with the promise of excitement.

Peering out the window toward the MacLeod lands, Moira worried her lower lip with her teeth. If she made her way to Errol herself, mayhap she could convince him in person. Enlisting his sister certainly hadn't helped.

Though she was sure her friend had tried. Just as Moira

would have tried if the roles were reversed.

"What has yer mind so occupied this morn?" Rory, her brother, asked from behind her.

She spun in surprise and caught his eyes moving in the direction she had been looking.

"'Tis naught that ye can help me with."

He frowned. "Mayhap, I can. Ye havenae e'en asked."

She laughed and rolled her eyes.

"Because I ken better. Dinnae ye have sword or archery practice to get to? Da willnae be happy to hear ye are shirking your training."

Rory had the gall to look appalled, leaning back with a palm placed over his heart. "I can best any man out there in the field. Da well kens that."

"But, whilst they train to improve, ye dinnae, so yer skills will remain stagnant. Soon, they will be besting ye, and then what will ye do?" she asked, crossing her arms in front of her.

"Well, Da doesnae expect me there today. I'll be hiking to the mountains later."

Moira perked up at that revelation. "Where?"

Her brother was an avid mountaineer. He loved being outside hiking and climbing mountains. If there was a sheer cliff, he'd be sure to scale it.

Rory looked at her suspiciously. "Why?"

She shrugged, keeping her face neutral. "Just curious, is all. Mayhap I would like to take up hiking."

"Nay. Absolutely no'." He wagged his finger at her. "I dinnae want to be responsible for ye scaling a mountain. Or a cliffside. Or e'en a hill for that matter."

She uncrossed her arms and pierced him with a glare. "Ye act as if I've no skill when it comes to those things."

He nodded. "Aye. Because ye dinnae." Turning on his heel, he left her to once again gaze out the window and try to come up with a plan that would get her from Hartsmoor and over to the MacLeod keep.

It wasn't safe for her to travel alone, yet she couldn't take anyone along with her. Her brothers and sisters couldn't be asked. Especially her sisters, Eilidh in particular. For certs she would run to their mother and tell her what Moira was up to.

She supposed she could take Seema, her maid, but she would be met with disapproval from her as well.

Then she thought of the frequent visitors, unaffiliated to a clan, that arrived at Hartsmoor all of the time. If she didn't dress in Hart colors and instead dressed like a village girl, it was possible that neither clan would pay her any attention as they wouldn't ken which clan she belonged to. They could assume that she belonged to one of the villages that remained neutral and unaffiliated. That would be her greatest chance of crossing onto MacLeod lands and getting to Errol.

As the plan formed in her mind, she tried not to think about her parents and siblings. Their reactions would be furious. If caught, her father would for certs lock her in her bedchamber with a guard posted at the door and not let her out until she was married off.

Moira shuddered at the thought.

She kenned her father was actively keeping his eyes and ears open for a good match for her. She was thankful that he was a caring man and would be very stringent in his choice. He ensured Moira that it would be someone whom she could see herself spending the rest of her life with, but she wasn't ready yet. She didn't want to be married at this time.

Her life was hers right now, as much as it could be anyway, and she enjoyed having her days—and nights—to herself.

Pushing away from the window with a sigh, she tried to come up with an excuse for her to leave the gates. She'd done it afore and had never had an issue. Why was she so hesitant this time?

Because she was traveling to the MacLeod lands. That's why.

If her parents were to find out they would be enraged with her. Her brothers, too.

Never mind the potential danger she was putting herself in. Not only herself, her family and clan as well.

It would have been best if Anna could have convinced Errol to help. Then they could have met halfway.

Moira wondered what her best friend was doing. She was grateful that her parents, along with Anna's father agreed, although with much ire, to allow them to remain friends. She didn't understand this constant need to be at odds with each other.

Long ago she'd asked her father what the reason was for the strife betwixt the two clans. He'd just shaken his head and shrugged as he shooed her away, telling her not to burden herself with such worrisome topics.

She'd long believed that the reason had been lost through the years since she could never get an answer.

A knock sounded at the door and Seema, her maid, entered.

"Seema. Is ma downstairs?"

"I believe she is in her drawing room with her maid and Morven. They are doing needlepoint."

Moira scrunched her nose. Of course, her youngest sister was at her mother's side. And doing needlepoint. She shuddered. It was a task she couldn't stand.

It was also one that she wasn't very good at. She would much rather be reading through the tomes in the family annals.

"'Tis a lovely day out and I fancy a walk through the woods," she announced.

Seema's eyes narrowed. "I ken that look. What are yer true plans?"

Moira shushed her and feigned offense. "Ye must admit it looks beautiful today."

"I will admit to no such thing," Seema drawled.

AN HOUR LATER Moira rode out of the gates, not toward MacLeod lands, but west, deeper into Hart lands. She didn't want to arise the suspicion of the guards keeping watch, and since she rode the lands often, none gave her a second look seeing the direction she was headed.

When she was satisfied she was far enough away from Hartsmoor, she pulled on the reins, slowing her horse to a stop. If she turned and headed northeast, she would eventually run into MacLeod territory.

Reaching for the bag she'd brought along, Moira withdrew the cloak she'd stuffed inside. Its colors belonged to neither Hart nor MacLeod. It would make traveling unnoticed much easier.

She slipped off her own cloak and shoved it into the bag, then pulled the other one on, securing it at her neck.

Looking up, she gauged the sun's location. It wasn't an easy task. The pine branches hung thick overhead and blocked much of what she was searching for, but she finally figured it out.

Happy with what she believed was the way to MacLeod lands, Moira steered the horse in that direction at a trot. Soon, she pushed the horse faster. Trees passed in a blur as she dodged low-hanging branches, taking care to keep her face scratch-free.

The sun was high in the sky. She would need to make haste if she expected to get to MacLeod lands and back afore nightfall.

Urging her horse on, she felt bad for pushing the creature to such lengths. Soon he would need to stop to rest a bit and drink.

A burn flowing with fresh water came into view and Moira slowed the horse, leading him to the water so he could drink his fill. Nearby, she dropped to her knees and splashed the cool water on her face. She studied her surroundings. Pine needles, orange with age, carpeted the forest floor beneath her. It felt as if she were kneeling upon a pillow.

The tangy scent of pine surrounded her, infiltrating her senses. Birds tweeted from the branches above, their happy birdsong echoing in the air, lightening her mood. She loved the freedom the woods offered. It was her second favorite place to be.

Moira had to be getting close to MacLeod lands. She'd been riding for what seemed like hours and her surroundings were unfamiliar. She was either on the thin strip of Mackenzie land that separated the Hart and MacLeod lands, or she'd crossed over onto MacLeod lands. She wasn't certain.

Her horse lifted its head, sniffing the air for a moment before turning its attention back to the burn and continued drinking.

The forest suddenly grew quiet and once again her horse stopped drinking. He huffed as he bobbed his head and stomped his hoof into the soft ground.

Unease flooded Moira and she held her breath, her gaze scanning the trees.

She couldn't see anything, but there was a reason why the critters stopped chattering.

Someone was watching her. She could feel it. She couldn't see them, but they were there.

She closed her eyes and took a deep breath, praying it was friend and not foe. Just in case, she slowly dropped her hand to clasp the dirk tucked into her boot.

"Dinnae move." The order came from a low voice, just over her right shoulder.

Moira froze, not daring to move at the gruff voice that ordered her to remain still. Her eyes widened at the feel of steel prodding her back. She didn't ken who it was, but she kenned very well when a sword was pointed at her.

"Whate'er ye are reaching for, I suggest ye stop," the man growled.

Moira sighed. "I am only traveling to meet friends. I've done naught." It wasn't a lie.

"Alone?"

She could lie. Though whoever accosted her would easily see through it. Mayhap if she didn't have her horse with her, she could make the tale believable. There would be more than one horse if she were traveling with someone else.

Cursing silently, she wished she could see who it was behind her. What clan they were affiliated with. Though with his dour countenance, for certs he was a MacLeod.

"Are ye traveling alone? I willnae ask again."

He prodded her shoulder with the tip of his sword again, and she flinched.

"Aye. I am visiting with friends."

"Ye should ken better than to be out here alone. Stand up and turn around."

Moira closed her eyes and took in a deep breath. The intentions of this man, whoever he was, were clear. What had she gotten herself into?

"Are ye daft? Must I keep repeating myself?"

Slowly, she stood and turned to face the man.

Not a MacLeod.

A Mackenzie. Not an enemy, but not necessarily an ally either.

She breathed a sigh of relief.

Until the man's gaze roved over her body like she was a meal, and he was starving. He licked his lips, a sneer transforming his face into something sinister.

He still had the tip of his sword pointing at her. Any move she made to grab her dirk would quickly be stopped with a stab. He would for certs catch her if she tried to run. The man was tall and lanky with long legs. He could easily take one stride for her three.

Moira refused to let him see her fear—even if it bubbled up within her, threatening to spill over. Instead, she straightened her shoulders and jutted out her chin, looking the man straight in the eye.

"Ye should take care and be on yer way," she said firmly.

"And ye should have taken care no' to travel alone."

Quickly he closed the distance betwixt them and Moira sucked in a breath. She had nowhere to run.

"I suggest ye stop harassing the lass."

The warning was clear, and the man who was so close to her

that she could smell his fetid breath, widened his eyes. He was blocking her view so she couldn't see who had delivered the command.

The Mackenzie spun and confronted the intruder. "The wench is mine. Go find yer own," he spat.

"Ye've no right to the lass that is clearly on my land. Leave now, afore I force ye."

The words he spoke sunk in. She wasn't on Mackenzie land. That could only mean one thing—she'd made it to MacLeod land.

Inwardly, she groaned. The new situation probably wouldn't fare any better for her.

The Mackenzie looked over his shoulder at her, his eyes narrowed and turned back to the MacLeod and spit on the ground at his feet.

"I'll concede as there is nay need for spilt blood today. But I make no promises for future encounters." With his parting words, he walked away, giving a wide berth to the man that had stood up for her.

Once he learned she was a Hart, his chivalry wouldn't last. She dared not look at the man for fear of his reaction. Moira could only hope that he would believe her to be a commoner and allow her on her way.

"What are ye doing on MacLeod lands?" He demanded, his voice as sharp as the sword that had been pointed at her chest just minutes ago.

"I am visiting friends," she murmured, deciding to keep the same excuse she'd used afore.

"We arenae expecting anyone. Show yer face."

His voice was firm. Unbending.

She didn't move.

"Are ye hurt?" Concern laced his question.

That was unexpected.

The man approached and she stiffened.

"Ye're safe. I willnae hurt ye, lass."

His voice was vaguely familiar. Could it really be who she

sought?

The man reached out and removed her hood. With his fingers on her chin, he forced her to look at him.

She rounded her eyes with recognition.

Errol.

Their gazes clashed and his pupils blew wide when he realized who she was.

"Shite," he cursed. "Are ye daft?"

Errol pushed away from her as if he had been burned.

She scrambled to her feet. "I-I need yer help."

"Did ye no' get Anna's message? I said nay." He scraped his hands through his short hair. "Jesus. Do yer brothers ken ye are here? Yer da?"

"Of course no'," she scoffed.

He groaned. "What have ye done?"

"Errol." She touched his arm, but he snatched it away. "I really do require yer assistance."

"There is naught that I can do for ye, that yer brothers cannae. Are ye trying to start a war?"

"Nay!" She crossed her arms defiantly. "Look. I can show ye why I cannae ask my brothers." She pulled the weathered map from her pocket and held it out to him.

He gave her a bored look and made no move to take the paper.

"Please. Just look at it. Ye will see why I need ye," she pleaded. Waiting, her breath hitched, she worried that he would turn around and leave her there.

With a sigh, he looked up to the sky and accepted the map. Unfurling it carefully, his eyes slid over the ancient writing. He studied it for a long time afore looking up.

"What is this?"

"A map," she offered.

He narrowed his eyes. "I can see that. Where did ye find it?"

"In the Hart annals. Da tasked me with putting e'erything in order. This was in a small cupboard dug into the stone behind an ancient shelf unit."

Errol handed the map back to her. "I cannae help ye."

"Ye must!" She couldn't help the tone of desperation that crept into her voice. "As ye saw, some of the map is on MacLeod lands. Alpin and Rory cannae help me there. Here. That is why I need yer assistance."

"Nay."

One word.

She hadn't traveled this far to be denied.

"The map promises a great treasure. I will share it with ye," she blurted.

He studied her face, and she felt small under his scrutiny. Errol MacLeod was a fierce warrior. Broad of shoulder, with massive arms like tree trunks. His size rivaled her older brother, Alpin. Both men were intimidating in their stature.

"I havenae time for silly games."

"Ye have seen it for yerself, Errol. 'Tis no' games or fodder."

She wasn't sure if she was convincing him, but she needed to try. If peace betwixt the clans was true as the map promised, she needed to find the treasure. The need to stop the constant battling driving Moira to insist on his help. The dream that the Harts and MacLeods could live in harmony was one she long strived for, but never thought possible. This was a glimmer of hope she had not kenned existed.

"I've seen no such treasure on MacLeod lands. Whate'er was there, for certs is long gone by now. I've no interest in a wild chase."

"Please, Errol. Do ye really believe whoe'er took the time to put this map together and went to such lengths to hide the items left them where they would be found easily?" She shook her head. "They wouldnae. Ye can have whate'er proves to be MacLeod treasure and I'll keep the Hart treasure."

"Yer brothers and da will have my head."

"They willnae find out."

"How do ye propose to keep it from them?"

She shrugged. "I havenae decided." Then she got an idea. "If I say I am having an extended visit with Anna, there will be no question."

He shook his head. "'Twill no' work. Ye need to return home."

"Please." One word. Moira realized she was begging at this point.

He closed his eyes as if he were in pain.

When he opened them, he pierced her with a glare.

"Fine. I will help, but I want sixty percent of the finding."

She wanted to jump up and cheer with his agreement to help her, but she remained calm. And in no way was she giving him sixty percent.

"Forty."

"Fifty," he countered.

She sighed. "Agreed," she said begrudgingly.

"Return home and figure out yer visit." He paused. "Ye rode here alone?"

"Of course."

He grumbled a few words about disobedient women and shook his head. "I will escort ye off MacLeod lands and through Mackenzie lands to ensure yer safety. Once ye are on Hart lands, I will return home."

She worried her bottom lip. "Ye dinnae need to do that. I got here just fine."

He raised a brow in question. "And what of the Mackenzie that was verra close to attacking ye?"

Och. Errol was right, of course.

"Just until I get to the Hart border."

As they mounted their horses and rode side by side in silence, Moira couldn't help but smile. She'd wanted to track Errol down and convince him to help her. She'd convinced him, but he found her first.

She slid her gaze over to him. His back was straight, eyes scanning the surrounding trees for danger. She kenned his ears were listening for the slightest noise that would alert him that something was amiss.

His rugged handsomeness kept her attention.

He must have felt the heat of her gaze, and he shifted his eyes to her. She quickly looked away.

"Thank ye for agreeing."

He harrumphed but didn't say anything. Just prodded his horse to a trot.

They remained quiet on the journey to Hart lands and when they arrived, he made a hasty retreat, heading back to his own keep.

Moira sat atop her horse watching until he disappeared through the thick trees.

She'd done it. She'd enlisted Errol's help.

Now, she only needed to convince her family to allow her to visit Anna for an extended visit.

That would be easier said than done.

HE WATCHED FROM a distance, hoping that the Mackenzie would finish what he'd started and go through with his plans. Ravish the Hart bitch and then slice her throat. He'd gladly watch.

Hell, he would make his way closer to her just so he could see the life ebb out of her eyes.

Biting back the laugh that threatened to escape from his lips, he held himself back and watched, irritated when Errol MacLeod appeared.

The Hart wench would live another day. As would the MacLeod son. He would be harder to deal with. The man was destined to be laird. He was well-trained. A warrior.

All the things he wasn't.

He'd never been trained in aught. Nay, his da had thought him useless.

He swiped his arm across his nose, wiping the snot that leaked from it. The blooming of all the trees set his nose off every spring season. It was just one more fault to add to his da's never-ending list of things that were wrong with him.

His brother, older by three years, had been perfect in every way.

The perfect son.

The perfect brother.

The perfect man to continue on ensuring the family secret remained uncovered.

But his brother was no longer here.

Neither was his father.

What would they say now that the possibility of the knowledge of their heritage was at risk of being kenned to both the Hart and MacLeod?

That he was the only one left to keep it secret?

Now that it was all left to the one considered a failure.

"I will be successful," he murmured, keeping his voice low, even though the pair had traveled far enough away that they couldn't possibly hear him.

Standing tall, he looked to the path where they'd disappeared afore turning back to make his way home. The unsteady sound of his footsteps an irritating reminder that he would always be lacking. The way he had to drag his left leg along to keep up with his right. The awkward limp it gave him. He remembered the way his father would look at him with disgust. As if he'd somehow brought his afflictions upon himself.

The old man thought he could beat his ailments out of him. "It didnae work for ye, though did it, Da?" He questioned the empty woods surrounding him. Waited for an answer that he kenned would never come.

Nay. He was the last one standing. The last of a dying family line.

But he would ensure their family secret didn't come to light.

CHAPTER FOUR

MACLEOD KEEP WAS similar in size to Hartsmoor Castle. It loomed tall and foreboding as the traveling party that escorted Moira for her visit approached.

It took a lot of convincing and begging to her parents for them to allow such a visit. Many messages were sent back and forth betwixt the two clans. Promises were made that no harm would come to Moira and Seema while they visited.

She had no doubt about that. The MacLeod weren't a cruel clan. And while she didn't think they and the Harts would ever be allies, they had come to a truce. One of many, of course, but neither clan had attacked the other in recent years.

Anna was waiting in the courtyard when they arrived. A huge smile splitting her face as she clapped her hands excitedly, hopping up and down.

When the carriage came to a stop, Moira jumped down and the two girls embraced. Errol was also there. Standing stoically to the side, watching them with a scowl on his face, saying naught.

She dropped into a curtsy in greeting, and then Anna grasped her hand and pulled her inside. Seema did her best to keep up.

"I cannae believe yer parents allowed this," Anna exclaimed. "It has been much too long."

"Me either." Moira giggled. "'Twasnae easy. But I'm here. Though 'tis only for a fortnight and a half." She dropped her voice. "Then I must return for a cousin's wedding."

"Who?"

"'Tis one of the southern Hart cousins." She sighed. "I dinnae ken why I must go. I have ne'er met her."

Errol entered, his cousin Robbie behind him glaring at Moira.

She shivered. He'd come to Hartsmoor afore, accompanying Laird MacLeod and Errol on their visits. He had a fierce look to him, and Moira wasn't convinced that the man actually kenned how to smile.

"Ignore them," Anna said. "Let us go up to my bedchamber and ye can tell me about yer plans."

Anna's bedchamber was on the second floor, to the right, and all the way down the hall. A bed, piled high with throws and furs stood in the center. A trunk at the foot of the bed was covered with a heavy blanket. The fireplace burned bright, the high flames licking up the stone hearth and disappearing up the chimney. A wooden table with chairs was set near a tapestry covered window.

"Yer trunk will be brought up soon, unless ye need it afore then?"

Moira waved her hand in dismissal. "Nay. No need."

They both sank onto the bed in a fit of giggles. "I am so glad ye are here." Anna sat up straight, a kenning look widening her eyes. "Does this visit have aught to do with yer letter asking for Errol's help?"

She should have kenned that it wouldn't take long for Anna to question her about that. Her friend was way too curious to let something such as that go without addressing it.

"I met him in the woods," Moira confessed.

Anna's eyes rounded. "Ye didnae!" She exclaimed.

"I did! No' purposely though. Well, I was planning on finding him, but he found me first."

"He hasnae mentioned any such meeting."

Moira giggled. "I'm sure he hasnae."

Her friend grew serious. "So," she looked around the room as if someone was there listening to their conversation and lowered her voice. "What is it that ye need Errol's help for? That yer brothers couldnae assist?"

"A treasure map."

Anna cocked her head. "Ye jest."

"I doonae. I found it hidden in the wall when I was putting the Hart annals to order."

Anna stood and paced the room. Then stopped in front of Moira. "So why would ye need Errol for that?"

With a sigh, Moira pulled the map from her pocket and unfurled it so Anna could look at it. She pointed her finger to a corner of the map.

"This part takes place on MacLeod lands. Without Errol's help I would ne'er be able to get to it."

Anna took the map and studied it, turning the paper and looking at it at different angles. "I wonder what the treasure is?"

"I dinna ken. It just says coins and a Hart family legacy." She shrugged. "I havenae any idea what that could be. Or why my family's legacy would be located on MacLeod land. But mayhap it could lead to peace."

"Hmm." Anna's teeth caught the corner of her bottom lip as she studied the map further. "That is an interesting turn of events. It doesnae make any sense truly."

"Exactly. Our families' pasts are quite tumultuous, though I dinnae ken why. I've e'en asked my father why, and he didnae have an answer he could give."

A knock sounded and a maid entered, carrying a tray of dried meats, crusty bread, and honey mead.

"Laird MacLeod has insisted that ye eat after yer long journey." She curtsied and left the room.

As if on cue, Moira's stomach rumbled loudly, and both girls laughed out loud.

They moved to the table and Anna poured two cups of the sweet drink.

Moira drank deeply, not realizing how thirsty she was. Then

she broke off a piece of bread and slathered it with fresh-churned butter. It was divine.

"I am still amazed that ye managed to convince Errol to help ye. How did ye do it?"

"I had to promise to share half the treasure with him," Moira grumbled.

Anna dipped her head to hide her smile. "That sounds like him." She straightened, growing serious. "Now that ye are here, how do ye plan to treasure hunt? That map seems to take ye further away from not only Hartsmoor, but also MacLeod Keep. It goes deep into the Highlands."

"Aye," Moira sighed. "'Twould be so much easier if I were a man. Then I wouldnae need to explain where I was going to be for e'ery minute of the day. But alas, I dinnae have such luxury. I will figure it out, though. I must."

"Whate'er ye need me to do, I will do it. Ye ken that, aye?"

Moira nodded thinking of how she could pull off such a feat. She was grateful to have such a good friend as Anna. There was no doubt that her friend would indeed do whatever it took so that she could go off on this adventure with Errol.

Because that's what it was. An adventure.

One that, once solved, hopefully both lairds would understand why she'd taken such drastic measures. Though her reasoning wasn't completely selfless. Aye, she wanted peace betwixt the clans, it would benefit all of their people. No more deaths from the fighting. Nor any more burned crofts and crops. No more stolen cattle and sheep. To have the answer from the past to whatever it was that caused the strife betwixt them solved, would be a blessing. But, selfishly, she wanted unobstructed access to her best friend.

They ate in silence for a few moments until Anna suddenly slapped her hand on the tabletop.

"I've got it!" She exclaimed excitedly.

Moira looked at her questioningly.

"I ken how to get ye and Errol on yer way."

"Aye? How?"

Anna nodded. "We can travel north. The weather has started to warm. A trip to take in our lands and enjoy some fresh air."

Moira frowned. "How does that help?"

"It gets us away from here and headed in the correct direction. Da will ne'er let ye both leave together for no reason. Howe'er, if ye and I are traveling, he will insist Errol attend to us." She shrugged. "Probably Robbie as well."

Moira shuddered. She wasn't happy with the addition of Robbie. He kept it no secret that he did not appreciate her presence at MacLeod Keep. She couldn't fathom how he would react to being forced to attend her travels.

Anna clapped her hands. "This will be such fun."

Moira wasn't so sure, but she was happy they had a plan.

TWO DAYS LATER, Moira was on a horse, Anna on her own horse at her side. Errol and Robbie rode ahead of them, both wearing frowns that said they would rather spend their days doing anything else than the trip that lay ahead.

Seema and Fina rode behind them, chattering away. She was glad to see that the two of them got on well together.

Moira studied Errol from behind and she wondered if he could feel the heat of her gaze on his back. His broad shoulders created an impressive visage. He sat tall atop his black horse with the perfect circle on its flank as he stared straight ahead and lead them out of the gates of the keep.

Surprisingly, it didn't take much to convince the laird to allow them to travel together. Moira had the suspicion that it was in the way Anna asked. Being the only lass in the family, Moira could see how all the men practically tripped over their own feet to do her bidding.

She couldn't relate to that type of treatment. She was far from being the only woman in her family, and thankfully, her mother was still with them.

Anna losing her mother at birth weighed heavily on the men in her life. They all tried to make up for it by giving her whatever she wanted.

"This is verra exciting," Anna said as she brought her horse close to Moira's.

Moira smiled at her best friend, and her brows drew together. Anna's color didn't look quite right. Her skin had turned pale, and she appeared tired.

"Are ye well?" Moira asked, concern lacing her voice.

"Aye. Why do ye ask?"

Moira got the impression that Anna wasn't being completely truthful. But she didn't want to push her friend if it was naught, so she waved it off. "Just making certs."

They rode deeper into the woods, Errol and Robbie ignoring them and their conversations. Their eyes were constantly scanning the woods for any trouble. Just because they were on MacLeod lands didn't mean that there weren't people with ill-intentions lying in wait.

Looking over at Anna, Moira's concern grew. Her friend's color had completely drained from her face, and she was barely staying astride.

"Errol," Moira called out. "We must stop."

"We still have a way afore we arrive at our first rest spot," he said gruffly.

"Yer sister cannae wait that long."

He didn't look back. Just kept moving forward and Moira thought he wouldn't respond.

"She will let me ken when she needs rest," he called over his shoulder.

"I dinnae think she is capable, she really—"

Just then Anna listed off her horse, falling to the ground below.

"Anna!" Moira called, rearing her horse to a stop and dropping down to help her friend. Her skin was heated under Moira's palms.

"Christ," Errol snapped, jumping off his horse to help his sister. "Why did ye no' say aught sooner?"

Moira rolled her eyes, but she could see the worry reflected in Errol's brown orbs.

He did a quick check of Anna's body making sure that she hadn't broken any bones.

Anna's eyes fluttered opened. "Why have we—" she grasped her stomach and turned to the side, expelling what she'd eaten early.

Robbie jumped back from where he was standing beside Anna to avoid the remnants of her retching. He moved to his horse and returned with a small square of linen for Anna to wipe her mouth.

"We need to turn back," Robbie said to Errol.

"Nay!" Anna called out, her head snapping up. "I feel better now. 'Twas just something I ate that didnae settle well."

Moira wasn't convinced. Her skin was a bit gray in color. Fina was rubbing her back, trying to comfort her, but Anna shrugged her off as if she didn't want the attention.

"I am well. I assure ye. Let us continue on."

Errol and Robbie exchanged glances and Moira kenned they were contemplating on whether they should turn back or not.

"Errol MacLeod, we will continue on this journey as planned," Anna stated, her voice sounding surprisingly strong.

Errol sighed and helped her atop her horse afore turning to Moira and doing the same. His large hands closed around her waist, sending heat through her body. She looked at him to see if he'd felt the same, but his jaw was set firm, and as soon as her bottom settled on her horse, he was gone.

Robbie helped Fina and Seema before sitting atop his own horse once again.

"Ye do ken that yer sister is unweel and should return home?" Robbie asked.

Errol's eyes jumped from his cousin and back to his sister. With a defeated sigh, he kicked his horse into a trot.

Robbie threw an irritated look back to them afore hurrying to catch up to Errol.

An hour later, they had to stop for Anna to vomit again. This time it wasn't only Anna. Fina dropped to her knees as well. Both of them emptying their stomachs.

Robbie was right. Moira was irritated that she agreed with the man, but he was right. Clearly, there was something amiss with Anna and Fina. They needed to be home so they could see the healer and get a tisane to stop the roiling of their stomachs.

"We should go back," Moira said to Errol. "Traveling willnae help them."

"I agree," Errol said, his brows drawn down in concern as he assessed his sister's pale skin and the way she clenched her stomach.

Fina was experiencing the same symptoms.

"Nay," Anna called out, her voice still surprisingly strong. "Fina and I will return. Ye and Errol must go forward," she insisted. "'Tis yer only chance to solve the riddle."

"I cannae possibly leave ye," Moira said.

Anna shook her head. "'Tis I that is leaving ye. As ye said afore, ye doonae have a lot of time to spend searching for yer treasure. Ye must go on. Robbie will escort us home."

Errol stiffened. "I cannae take Moira alone. Her father and her brothers will have my head. Hell, our father will have my head."

"Dinnae be silly," Anna answered, waving her hand weakly in dismissal. "Ye will have Seema with ye and besides, time is of the essence. I will take care of father, and the Hart's will be none the wiser when she returns with the treasure."

Errol squeezed the bridge of his nose and Moira held her breath as she waited for his response.

She approached Anna and clasped her hand. "I shouldnae leave ye when ye arenae well. What kind of friend would that make me?"

"One with a mission. Ye are so close, dinnae let me be the one to stop ye. I will be cheering ye on from MacLeod Keep and will be the first one to greet ye upon yer return." She squeezed Moira's hand in encouragement. "Truly, 'tis naught but an unsettled stomach. Fina and I had the same food when we broke our fast, mayhap it was spoilt."

Moira had a hard time believing that she and Fina both ate spoiled food, or that it was even a probability.

"Go. Ye are wasting the day. Robbie will take good care of us on our journey back."

In answer, Robbie harrumphed but nodded.

Errol opened his mouth to say something, but Anna held up a hand and stopped him.

"Go," she demanded. "I shallnae say it again. Ye both have my blessing. We will be fine."

Finally, after more discussions back and forth, the two parties split and went their separate ways—Anna, Robbie, and Fina back to MacLeod Keep, and Moira, Errol, and Seema headed deeper into the trees.

Errol's mouth was a thin line as Moira urged her horse forward to catch up to him and settled into a rhythm beside him.

"I dinnae ken if ye have thought about how to get to the first location on the map, but there seemed to be a path through a copse of trees. It should lead us right to it."

Errol's gaze slid to hers. "Why would it be so straightforward? For certs if it were that easy, then the treasure has already been uncovered."

Moira rolled her eyes and chewed on her fingernail as she thought about what he said. "Dinnae ye think it would be well-kenned if it had been found? 'Tis promising treasure untold and a Hart family legacy."

Errol scoffed. "No' if it was someone other than a Hart that found it. Would ye go around yelling to the world that ye found a MacLeod treasure?"

She blew out an exasperated breath. He had a point, though she would never admit it and give him the satisfaction.

Retrieving the map from the bag she'd looped over her shoulder, she studied its contents. "We should be arriving soon, aye?" They'd been riding for what seemed like hours. Her bum was sore. She needed to relieve herself and stretch her legs.

"Can we stop for a few minutes?"

"Why?"

She sighed. The man was obtuse.

Handsome, but stubborn. Though she would never confess to either.

"If ye must ken, I need to attend to personal matters. I am for certs that Seema must as well."

"I thought ye said we should be there soon."

"I didnae say that actually. I *asked* ye. Which ye ignored, by the way."

"Fine. But be quick about it. I dinnae want to spend the night outside if we can help it."

Moira and Seema made their way past some young saplings. A boulder offered privacy from Errol, though he was paying them no attention.

"Ye mustnae push him so, my lady. Do ye forget that he is doing ye a favor by agreeing to this journey?"

"Nay, but he can be more accommodating, dinnae ye think?"

Seema shook her head and held back a giggle. "Both of ye are going to butt heads this whole journey."

"Why do ye say such a thing?"

"'Tis easy to see. Ye both are too similar. Ye shall see. I fear this will prove to be a verra long journey indeed."

A branch snapped in the distance and Moira froze, her gaze sweeping to Seema. "Did ye hear that?" She whispered.

Seema nodded.

Moira scanned the trees. She couldn't see aught out of the ordinary. She stood and ran her hands along her skirts to smooth them.

"'Tis more than likely an animal. Mayhap a deer. They blend into the trees so well."

"Aye," Seema agreed. "Let us return to Mr. MacLeod just to be safe."

When they emerged from the woods to where Errol waited by the horses, he held out a skin to Moira. "Ale. Ye should drink something," he remarked.

She accepted and took a long pull from the skin afore handing it to Seema. Her maid took a small sip and returned it to her. Handing it back to Errol, she said, "Thank ye."

"Ready to continue?" He asked gruffly.

With a sigh, she rolled her eyes and nodded. His reaction was as if they had just spent hours in the woods, putting them dreadfully behind schedule.

They rode on in silence, Errol's jaw set stubbornly.

She didn't understand why he was acting the way he was.

He was getting half of her treasure after all.

IT WOULD BE so easy to pluck the women off from his current vantage point. They had no awareness of how close to danger they were. Even easier as they would be caught unawares in a vulnerable position.

But now wasn't the time and he had to choose his actions wisely. Attack when it would be most advantageous to him and most detrimental to them.

Thankfully, the traveling party had been cut in half. With the MacLeod wench and her maid being overtaken by some ague that made them continuously upchuck, it really put them out of him having to fash about them. They would not cause any trouble.

And now that they'd returned to MacLeod Keep, he could concentrate on the three left.

Errol was posing a problem though. The man was a keen tracker. He kenned exactly when someone followed. When someone was near.

His eyes were always trained on the woods. Watching.

His ears were always tuned into the land and trees surrounding them. Listening.

The two women talked nonstop as if they hadn't a care in the world. Which was good for him. Their incessant babble acted as a buffer to any missteps he took.

But, more than once, he'd attracted Errol's attention.

Even with how careful he'd been, he'd made mistakes.

Like getting too close to the women right now. He could hear them as they relieved themselves. The soft trickle falling onto the pine needle covered ground.

He'd made the mistake of not paying attention and stepped on a twig. It cracked loud enough for them to give pause. He'd froze, afraid to even breathe for fear that they would see him.

They didn't though. Instead, believing they were perfectly safe, they likened the noise to a roaming animal and moved on.

Something his father would have done.

"I will keep our secrets. No one will ken about what our family has done," he whispered.

It had been a secret that they'd kept safe for generations. Passed down through the years.

But none of them were aware of the treasure hunt that had been hidden away. A hunt that alluded to sins of the past, he was sure. He needed to stop Errol and Moira from reaching the last clue. It would ruin everything.

He's lucky that he'd caught wind of their conversation when they spoke of what she'd found and their plans to uncover it.

He couldn't let that happen.

Refused to let it happen.

Last in their family or not.

Their secret would die with him.

◆———————◆

CHAPTER FIVE

T HEIR JOURNEY WAS off to a rough start. Their party had been cut in half and they weren't even through the first day.

Moira had been talking incessantly. It was as if she didn't need to breathe air. He just wanted a few moments of silence.

He was beginning to think that Robbie got the better end of this deal with being able to return to the keep.

Finally, their destination came into view.

As the map illustrated, a copse of trees lay ahead, an old worn path leading right down the middle of them and disappearing into the darkness beyond.

He looked over at Moira as they approached, her mouth forming a small 'o'.

"'Tis just like the map stated," she whispered.

"Aye."

She spurred her horse forward, and he cursed.

"Moira, slow yer approach!" He commanded. Who kenned what waited for them beyond the trees. He still wasn't fully convinced that this wasn't some sort of trap, but seeing how his sister was supposed to accompany them, that was more unlikely.

Moira would never put the life of her friend in danger.

Pulling on the reins, she slowed the horse and spun around to him.

"Why are ye lingering?"

"Ye dinnae ken what lies ahead."

"Aye, I do. Trees. A path. They lead to something. I dinnae ken what yet, but I will soon if we keep moving."

"Ye need to hold back," he ground out. "Let me take a look around to make sure 'tis safe."

Moira scoffed. "Surely ye jest? We have been riding for hours and have no' come across another soul."

"Well, mayhap they are all waiting at the destination?" Errol snapped. He couldn't help it. Moira Hart got under his skin. And not in a good way. She was like a splinter. The more you tried to pluck it out, the deeper it burrowed itself into your skin until it festered and bothered you enough that you wanted to do naught more than dig it out with your knife.

"Dinnae be silly. We would have heard something if that were the case."

"No' if they are stealthy. Trained. A man could wait in silence, undetected for hours, until his target came into view."

"Highly unlikely."

"Scouts do it all the time. Archers do it."

"Aye, to guard the keep," she said, exasperation lacing her voice. "Clearly no one has been here in a verra long time. And there is naught to guard."

He raised his brows. "If there is naught to guard then why are we here?"

She blew out a breath. "Stop twisting my words. Ye are just as annoying as my brothers." Stopping her horse, she crossed her arms and shot him a kenning look. "Go on." She waved in the direction of the path. "Check whate'er 'tis that is waiting to strike us down," sarcasm dripping from her words.

He dismounted and stalked up to her horse. "Ye think I am just like yer brothers? Well, ye are just like my sister, except with her, I can give in to whate'er she wants. I've no such obligation to ye, Lady Hart."

Errol had said the words with more vitriol than he intended, but lord above if the lass didn't niggle at his nerves.

He unsheathed his sword and started toward the path. "Stay where ye are until I clear the area."

It wasn't twenty seconds later when he felt a presence at his back and spun, sword out and ready to strike.

Moira gasped, putting her hands up. "'Tis just me."

He clenched his jaw as he quietly counted to ten in his head, hoping for patience. "I told ye to wait," he ground out.

"Aye, but as I said, why? There is no one here."

"We dinnae ken that yet."

"Ye are insufferable."

"Ye are intolerable."

She smiled at that, as if it was the biggest compliment he could offer her.

"Will ye please just wait a few minutes so I can do a cursory look?"

"Nay. I'm no' letting ye get to the clue first," she said stubbornly.

"Christ, woman. That is the last thing I am concerned with."

She shrugged, an irritated look on her face. "Hurry up, then. Ye yerself said ye wanted to ensure we are able to find a place to sleep indoors this night. The longer ye dally around, the longer 'twill take us to seek shelter."

"I dinnae dally."

Her laughter was loud enough to warn anyone of their approach—that is if their fighting back and forth hadn't alerted them already.

"It seems to me like ye are dallying."

Damn it. The lass was insulting. Along with being insufferable. And he couldn't forget incorrigible. How the hell did her brothers deal with her? It made sense to him now why they sent her away for almost a month. They were probably enjoying the peace and quiet.

"Be silent," he commanded in a loud whisper.

That stopped her laughter. She narrowed her blue eyes at him, crossed her arms, shot out a hip, and pursed her lips. Her annoyance was palpable.

Good.

Now, they were even.

"Stay here. I mean it this time. Believe it or no' 'tis for yer own safety."

Errol didn't give her time to answer, and he continued on the path. It was soon clear that it was just the three of them here. Brush and needles piled high, littering the path, along with dead leaves from several years past. This area of land hadn't been stepped upon in years. Still, the two women were in his care, and he would perform his due diligence to ensure their safety.

The path led through another archway of trees and then opened up to a long-abandoned castle. Errol looked at it with awe. He had no idea of its existence.

"Wow," Moira sputtered behind him.

Rolling his eyes, he huffed out a breath and pinched the bridge of his nose. It was impossible for her to listen to directions. Clearly, her will was too strong and she was going to do as she pleased, no matter what he said.

""Tis impressive, I must agree."

Together they walked toward the front of the old structure. The stone walls were crumbling. The rock worn smooth from the rain and wind.

"Take care, it could be dangerous," he warned.

"What's it called?" She asked.

He shrugged. "I dinnae ken. 'Tis obvious it hasnae been inhabited for years."

Moira paused. Her eyes scanned the landscape. "If I was a clue to treasure, I wonder where I would hide?" She tapped her finger on her chin. "How should we proceed? Split up? With the three of us it will go quickly."

"I think we should stay together." He gave her a stern look and crossed his arms, shutting down any chance for debate."

"Ye are the one who said that ye wanted to ensure we were able to sleep at an inn this night. Why wouldnae ye want us to each take a section to search?"

He pierced her with an irritated look and then moved his gaze to Seema who stayed behind Moira. He was certain that the maid was holding back a laugh.

Errol did not find any amusement in the situation.

"The longer ye stand here fighting me on this," Errol ground out, "the more chance that ye'll be spending yer night on the ground instead of a bed."

Moira harrumphed. "Fine. Let's all stay together," she called out loudly as if she had an audience outside of the three of them.

She trudged along beside him, mumbling under her breath, as they approached the rotting wooden door. She paused, holding up her hand.

"Afore we go inside, we should assess the outside. See what structures still stand."

Errol grunted, not because he disagreed, but because he didn't want Moira to ken that he agreed with her.

"Let us go right first," Moira ordered and headed to the right.

Around the corner was what Errol assumed was once a flourishing garden. Now it was overgrown with weeds standing as tall as him. In the far corner was a small hut, the thatched roof had given way long ago and had collapsed inside.

Moira quickened her pace as she walked excitedly to the shack.

Of course, she did.

"Lass, take care. It could be dangerous."

She paused with her hands on her hips and gave him a droll look. "'The roof has already collapsed. How much more dangerous can it be?" She spun and continued on.

Seema hurried past Errol, giving him an apologetic smile.

"Does yer mistress always disobey orders?" Errol asked.

The maid paused and looked to Moira afore answering. When her eyes met his, they crinkled at the corners. "Aye. Most especially when she is determined like she is now."

He hummed but said naught further as he trudged behind the

women.

The force of the collapsed roof had knocked the door off its frame. Peering inside they could only see the remnants of wet and mildewed straw. The musty smell tickled his senses, and he fought back a sneeze, squeezing the tip of his nose.

"We willnae find aught here."

"Ye doonae ken that. What if 'tis buried under all the hay?"

Errol frowned. He hoped not.

"Mayhap, but 'tis the first building. Let's see what else is here and search those."

When she moved away from the door to continue walking the parameter, Errol sent up a silent prayer of thanks. He had a feeling that he oft was going to regret agreeing to help Moira on her quest for treasure. No matter how much of the bounty, if there even was one, he was going to get.

He watched the sway of her arse as she walked in front of him. The lass was tiny, but her bottom was full and round. Of all the things Errol should be thinking about, Moira's body wasn't one of them.

As if he needed to give her brothers another reason to kill him. They would be furious enough once they found out he was traipsing along the countryside with their sister. He would never hurt the lass. Or act untoward to her. He had enough willing lasses to warm his bed that he wasn't so desperate to bed Moira.

Though he wouldn't turn her away.

Jesus. He needed to derail his thinking.

"Hello!" Moira snapped her fingers to catch his attention. "Are ye listening?"

"What?" he grumbled.

"'Tis a chapel."

They'd made their way to the other side. A pair of worn stone steps led to a stone archway. Surprisingly, the archway appeared to look stable.

"This is amazing, is it no'?" Moira breathed, walking through the arched entry, her blue eyes scanning the structure. She spun around, a huge smile on her face. "I have a good feeling about this chapel."

When they entered, he noticed the antechamber was tiny. Simple. The space couldn't hold more than eight people and that would be a stretch. A small pulpit that had been knocked over laid on the ground, the stone broken into two pieces.

Moira ran her hands along the walls. Tattered tapestries hung from rusted hooks. Some so threadbare, they'd broken from their hangers and fallen onto the floor. On the far wall, a stained-glass window let in faded colored rays of sunlight.

Errol held back as he watched Moira methodically search the tiny space. Moving around the fallen pulpit, she sought out the treasure but came back empty handed.

Straightening her back, she tucked her plump bottom lip under her teeth.

"It appears there's naught here. Mayhap we should move to the main building," Errol suggested.

Moira held up her hand. "No' so fast. When I found the map, it was in an alcove carved into the stone. It would make sense that mayhap whate'er 'tis we search for would be the same, no?"

He shrugged. "I suppose. But dinnae ye think that such a thing would have been discovered already?"

"Look how long it took me to find the map? How many generations afore me had been in that same room? Stared at those same walls? They had ne'er found it."

He couldn't argue with her logic. And that irritated him further.

"Check behind e'erything that is hanging. Or places where it appears something was hung afore."

Errol had to admire Moira's tenacity. Her attention to detail. The practical way she approached the search.

They each took a wall and began searching. He focused half of his attention on the wall, and the other half watching Moira out of the corner of his eye. She was methodical, her brows creased in concentration as she searched, her hands running along the wall. Her fingertips dipping into every crack and crevice.

He shook his head to clear his thoughts. Did he even ken if this hunt was not some far-fetched, elaborate plan to trap him? It was still possible. Moira and Anna's relationship he understood. They were the same age and were naive when it came to clan matters.

The question at hand was if Moira was as naive about them as she was letting on? Or was she luring him into a false sense of normalcy so that he would let his guard down and then pounce?

All he kenned was that he didn't have a choice. He would need to keep a keen eye out for what was happening around him.

"I'm no' finding aught," Seema announced and leaned against the wall she'd just searched.

Not wanting to give up, Moira asked her to move onto the next wall and search it the same way.

Errol spun to search another area, but the toe of his boot caught on something, and he lurched forward, steadying himself so he didn't fall.

"What did ye trip on?" Moira asked, ceasing her search and scanning the floor where he tripped.

"A loose rock, methinks."

But Moira was staring at the floor, shaking her head.

"Nay, not a stone at all." She dropped to her knees and swept her hand over the ground.

She continued to sweep until the residue and dirt was cleared from the section.

"Look, the square is loosened and lifting at the corner." She reached into her boot and withdrew a small blade. She stuck it under the lifted corner and tried to pry the heavy slate up.

Errol dropped down beside her and curled his fingers under the edge and pulled. Wiggling it back and forth a few times to dislodge it from the compacted dirt surrounding it, he finally was able to pull the slate away.

All three of them gasped in unison at what lay beneath.

"I'll be damned," Errol whispered, actually in awe that they found something. Mayhap Moira was being truthful about her quest. Mayhap. He still wasn't fully convinced.

"It's the same type of door that I found in Hartsmoor—only smaller," Moira whispered. "And dirtier." She yanked at the door, but it didn't budge.

It was more than likely stuck or rusted shut after all these years. He grabbed his dagger and using the handle as a mallet, he struck at the latched handle. It broke and they cleared away the iron.

Moira tugged and the door gave away, revealing a small cupboard.

The space looked too small to house anything, but when she pulled her hand out of the space, her fingers were curled around a small bundle.

With a huge smile on her face, her eyes clashed with his. Her brow raised defiantly. Almost in challenge. As if she was telling him that she kenned something would be here.

"What is it?" Seema asked quietly, excitement lacing her voice.

Moira blew away the thick layer of dust covering the bundle, and Errol waved his hands through the air to clear it away.

Untying the delicate string, she set it aside, then carefully unfolded the material surrounding whatever was inside.

Her brows furrowed as she stared at what she'd uncovered, her lips dropping into a frown.

"Is it a dead wee beastie?" Seema asked, taking a step back.

Moira rolled her eyes. "Now Seema, why would someone take such care for something like that? Nay, 'tis two miniature coats of arms."

She held them up so they could all see.

"Hart and MacLeod." Errol said, recognizing the emblems of both clans. "Why the hell would someone hide away our coats of arms together?"

CHAPTER SIX

MOIRA COULDN'T BELIEVE her luck. The hunt was real. Not some fool's chase that would lead to naught.

She looked at Errol and could see the disbelief on his face. She kenned he thought she had been telling tall tales when she first approached him with the map and the treasure. He was skeptical. The more she thought on that, she couldn't really fault him. He had no reason to believe aught that she said.

But with these two tiny pieces, she felt like she'd proven a point. They were made of silver, she was sure of it. The symbols from each of their clan's coat of arms were pressed into the metal.

It made no sense that they would be hidden away together.

"We should go. We can make it to the nearby inn to sup." Errol said, pushing up from the ground beside her.

"I will make sure our things are still in order." Seema rushed out the door and Moira found herself alone in the chapel.

Now that she'd found what she had been searching for, she took in the beauty of the old chapel. Afore it was a ruin, it must have been beautiful.

She should go so she can meet up with Seema and Errol and they can make their way to the inn afore continuing on to the next place on the map. She could picture colorful tapestries decorating the walls. Velvet runners covering the table and altar. It would have looked grand for certs.

As she stood, the small cubicle she'd opened earlier caught her attention. She looked around, but she was alone.

Reaching inside, she pulled another item. It was a small scroll of parchment. Fighting the temptation to read it here, she shoved it into her pocket, unsure if she wanted to share it with the others. She would read it first and then decide whether she would or not.

Errol popped his head inside. "Are ye coming?"

"Aye."

Her eyes swept the space one more time for aught she may have missed and then she slipped outside.

"Where's Seema?"

Errol shifted from one foot to the other, looking uncomfortable, before finally saying, "In the trees." He cleared his throat and quickly turned his attention back to his horse.

Moira rolled her eyes. Was it really that difficult to say she was attending to her personal matters? She did not understand how when men had no issue talking so bawdy amongst themselves. She'd heard plenty of conversations betwixt her brothers and other men in Hartsmoor. They were crude in their speech and vulgar in some of the movements used to express what they spoke of.

They waited a few minutes more but when Seema didn't emerge from the tree line, Moira looked at Errol uncertainly. "Do ye think she is well?" She asked.

Errol's brows drew together as he unsheathed his sword. "Would it matter if I told ye to stay here while I check?"

She crossed her arms. "Ye ken verra well that I am going to follow ye. She's my friend. I need to ensure her safety."

"She's yer maid."

True. She was. But Moira also considered Seema a friend. They had practically grown up together. And when Seema became an age where she needed to find a position, Moira had insisted that she be assigned to her. Not because she wanted to be waited on hand and foot. She didn't. But having Seema by her side for everything meant that their friendship could continue.

And it had. Though they did have to follow the societal norms and positions warranted by their statuses. Never once did it dampen their friendship and Moira was forever grateful for that.

"Friendships can be borne from spending so much time together. But, alas, Seema and I were friends long afore she became my maid."

He grunted. As if the idea was preposterous.

"Stay by my side and doonae run ahead."

Moira rolled her eyes but did as she was told.

Walking to the trees, Moira tried to peer through the thick brush and beyond, into the darkness of the forest.

It didn't take them long to find Seema. She was doubled over, clutching her stomach and Moira rushed to her side.

"Seema!" She cried, dropping to her knees beside her. "What has happened?"

Seema answered by turning away and retching onto the leafy ground.

"Och, have ye the same affliction as Anna and Fina?"

Seema didn't speak, but weakly nodded.

"Can ye ride?" Moira asked. They needed to get her to the inn and mayhap call for a healer.

Errol approached and gently lifted Seema off the ground and carried her to her horse, helping her settle atop and ensuring she was secured and wouldn't topple over.

"I dinnae think she should ride alone. She doesnae look steady. I fear she'll hurt herself further." He lifted her again and moved her to his horse.

Moira's eyes widened. "For certs, ye doonae expect her to ride with ye?"

He gave her a droll look. "Do ye have a better idea? She cannae ride with ye. If she falls o'er, ye both go down. She'll be safe riding with me."

Moving to Moira, he helped her mount her own horse. When

everything was secured and he tied a lead from Seema's horse to his own, he urged his horse forward, and Moira followed.

Worry had her chewing the inside of her cheek. Their luck had been both good and bad. Aye, they found the first, and maybe, second clue. But more than half of their original party had fallen ill with some sort of affliction. She hoped Anna and Fina were recovering well. And wished the same for Seema.

As they rode, no one else crossed paths with them, until they arrived in the village. Suddenly, the landscape was bustling with people moving to and fro. Selling food and wares from carts lined up along the buildings.

Moira noticed the looks they were receiving, and a sliver of wariness slid down her back. She supposed it must strike them as odd to see a MacLeod and a Hart traveling together. They both wore the colors of their clans. But no one approached them as they made their way to the small inn and that put her at ease.

They stopped their horses at the small stable off to the side of the main building. Two young lads rushed forth to take their horses. "Feed and bathe them well." Errol ordered and tossed them each a coin. Their eyes lit up as they bobbed their heads.

"They will have the best, my laird."

Moira found it interesting that Errol didn't correct them at the mistitle. Instead, he was concentrating on getting Seema inside along with their bags.

"Can ye walk, lass?" He asked gently.

Moira rushed forward to help Seema steady herself.

"I can," she answered, but grasped Moira's arm in a death grip so she didn't fall.

Arms laden with all their travel bags, Errol led the way inside where they were greeted by a cheery, old man.

He smiled warmly and welcomed them inside. His demeanor changed when he looked at Seema, worry creasing his brow afore focusing on Errol.

"We need a room and to sup." His eyes slid to Seema. "And a healer if ye ken of one?" Errol asked.

The man nodded and snapped his fingers. Another young lad stepped forward and then ran out the door to fetch the healer.

Grabbing two of the bags the man headed up the stairs, motioning for them to follow. "I've only the one room available and there is only one bed." He looked over his shoulder.

"That is fine," Errol answered as if it were natural.

Moira's heart skipped a beat as they entered the room where they would be spending the night. There truly was only one bed and it wasn't large enough for three. She looked nervously at Errol, but he was engrossed in conversation with the innkeeper at the room's door.

She led Seema over to the bed and helped her lay down.

"Mayhap the healer can give ye a tisane to ease the roiling of yer belly," Moira said hopefully, pulling off Seema's boots.

Seema groaned. "A healer is no' needed. I doonae think I can eat or drink aught right now. The mere thought makes me want to retch."

"Och, dear. That cannae be good."

Her maid patted her hand. "Just let me rest for some time. Ye and Errol should go sup. 'Tis been too long since ye've last eaten. Ye need all yer strength for yer adventures." Her mouth lifted in a smile that didn't quite reach her eyes. Her skin, usually rosy-cheeked and bright, was a sickly gray.

"I dinnae believe we will continue. We cannae. I need to make sure ye are feeling better."

"Ye must continue on, Moira," Seema said, her voice surprisingly strong. "Ye dinnae have a lot of time to solve the mystery that ye've only just begun to uncover. I will be fine. I am for certs 'twas just something that I ate."

Moira admired her friend's determination, but she couldn't leave her here alone at the inn to fend for herself. What kind of friend would that make her? Not a caring one, when the opposite was true.

Seema gave her a gentle shove. "Go now. Eat yer fill and stay strong."

"I dinnae think I should leave ye." Moira repeated, but Seema was insistent.

"I will still be here once yer stomach is filled."

Errol entered the room and his eyes slid to Seema. "Are ye feeling any better, lass?"

"My belly has settled. No' enough for me to eat, but 'tis feeling better."

"I am glad to hear that." His deep timbre sounded genuine, and Moira eyed him.

She was conflicted when it came to Errol. He was gruff and moody. Sometimes short and curt with his words. Then other times, he surprised her. He removed the bite from his voice, and it became warm and caring. Like sweet honey. She found she much preferred his attention when he looked at her with heat in his gaze. He hid it well. But once in a while she caught a glimpse and it made her belly do a tumble. A most peculiar feeling indeed.

A soft knock sounded, and Errol let the healer walk into the room. She was an elderly woman with a slight hunch to her back. Her gray hair was pulled back into a bun and tucked under her white head covering. She walked with a slight limp and looked as if every bone in her body ached.

Moira rushed forward. "Thank ye for coming on such short notice."

The woman gave her a quick nod and approached the bed where Seema rested. She poked and prodded at Seema's stomach. Felt her forehead. Her fingertips nimbly moved along her jawline and down her neck. Seemingly satisfied, she patted Seema on the shoulder and straightened—as best she could anyhow.

"Yer friend will be fine in a few days. Though my recommendation is that she no' travel in that time."

Moira nodded and said her thanks. As the woman exited, Errol placed some coins in her palm. She gave a small smile and disappeared into the hall.

"I told ye it was naught to fash o'er," Seema said. "I just need to rest. Which I will do once ye two leave to sup. Go on. I willnae stand for ye to go hungry in my presence." When neither she nor Errol made a move. She sighed. "I promise ye I will be fine. Please go."

"Come on, lass. Yer maid is correct. Ye need to sup. Let her rest awhile."

They both were right, of course, but it didn't dissipate the feeling of guilt wringing Moira's gut. When she looked at Seema, her maid nodded her head, encouraging her to go.

Moira clasped her hands together. "Lead the way," she said, trying to infuse some cheeriness into her voice.

Shortly after the two of them were seated at a table in the pub that was next door to the inn. It was crowded and filled mostly with men. Unless the serving wenches counted. Their low-cut gowns offering the men a glimpse of their bosoms.

Uneasiness settled in her belly. She didn't ken if it was because she was nervous from all the men surrounding her or if she was feeling the beginning of the affliction that had affected the others.

Most of the patrons wore the colors of the MacLeod clan, but not all. However, she noted no one wore the colors of the Harts. Moira fidgeted in her seat. People weren't outwardly staring at her, but she still felt a sense of anxiety. After all she was surrounded by clans people that her own family had been fighting against off and on for years.

"Ignore them," Errol spoke, drawing her attention. "They willnae harm ye. 'Tis more curiosity that sparks their interest."

She scanned the crowd. She wasn't so sure she agreed with Errol's assessment. Still, she wouldn't let them see her unease. She willed herself to stop her nervous fidgeting and by the time one of the serving wenches came to their table, Moira had somewhat calmed down.

Venison stew was on the menu for this evening and the server returned a few minutes later with two steaming bowls of stew filled to the rim. The thick liquid threatening to topple over the edge. An end of crusty bread was dunked into each bowl. The scent swirled around them, and Moira took a deep breath of the divine smell as the bowls were set in front of them. Two tankards of ale followed a few moments later.

"So, what is next on your quest?" Errol asked, before he took a huge bite of the bread that had been soaked in the stew.

Moira dug out the map and slid it over to him. "I'm no' for certs." She bit her lip and pondered whether or not she should disclose the parchment she found. She hadn't had a chance to read it yet so had no idea what it said. It could be a clue to where they need to go next.

Or it could be naught.

If it was something to assist their search, it would be daft of her to keep it a secret.

"I must confess, I havenae been completely honest," she said quietly.

Errol's head snapped up, his eyes narrowing, his mouth set in a thin line. Then he surprised her by sweeping his gaze over at the people in the pub, before turning his eyes back to her. His hard expression gave her naught and she wasn't sure why he looked so upset with her.

Still, she pushed on. Swallowing the lump that formed in her throat, she spoke. "After ye left the chapel earlier, I found another item in the cupboard."

His shoulders relaxed a little and his frown lifted just a bit.

"What was it?"

Moira lifted a shoulder in a shrug. "I dinna ken. 'Tis a scroll, but I havenae opened it to see what it says inside, if aught." She dug into her pocket and withdrew the rolled parchment.

"Open it." Errol leaned in, closing the distance between them, his curiosity piqued.

She slipped off the fragile twine keeping the paper rolled, and carefully unfurled it. The parchment looked similar to the map.

The ink faded from the passage of time. Moira had to squint her eyes to see.

Errol grabbed the candle and moved it closer so they could

read the words under more light.

> *'If ye are reading this, then ye have found our symbols.*
> *Two clans. Two coats of arms. One love.*
> *Continue yer quest for more.'*

Below the words was an illustration of what she could only assume was the next location.

Moira's gaze clashed with Errol's. "Are ye aware of a relationship betwixt a Hart and a MacLeod?"

Errol shook his head.

She didn't ken of one either. She only kenned that the riff between the clans had started long ago. Long afore her da was born.

"But, clearly, that is what this is saying is it no'?"

Rubbing the stubble of his beard, he shrugged. "I cannae disagree, but I ken of none."

Were they following some sort of love quest? Nay, they couldn't be. The map mentioned a hidden Hart treasure. That wouldn't equate to some lover's tryst equating to a treasure hunt.

But she was baffled. In all of her research she had never found aught to suggest that the Harts and MacLeods had ever come together in a union. It would have been in the Hart annals. For certs her parents would have been aware of such a coming together. Wouldn't they?

"If we continue on, the next stop on the map is a day's ride from here."

Her head snapped up. "Ye ken the location? Is it still on Mac-Leod lands?"

"Aye. I ken the general area. Though I dinnae remember what is there."

THE FIRST CLUE had been found. Just as he believed, this hunt would uncover what his family had fought so hard to keep quiet for generations.

As much as he wanted to cut them down where they had stood at the chapel, he took pause at committing such an unholy act on sacred ground. His hesitation made no sense, really. He didn't really believe in a higher power. If there was someone in the clouds, dictating people's livelihoods from above, then they for certs would not have assigned him this particular lot in life. Why make him suffer for untold reason?

But it mattered naught. It was too soon. He needed to wait until they got to the last clue afore making his move. That way he could destroy all the clues, and no one would be the wiser.

His mission would be complete. His family's secret would remain buried.

"I told ye I was smart," he snapped to his father.

The man's voice still rang strong in his head. Telling him he would be naught. That he was the reason his mother was dead.

Part of that was true, he supposed. She had died whilst birthing him. But was that really his fault? He had no control over such happenings. Mayhap she was a weak woman.

His brother had tried to talk about their mother. As if such conversations would keep her alive in their minds.

'Twas foolhardy. He had never met the woman. Never seen her. There was naught to remember.

He continued to watch them as they discussed their plans on how they would get to the next location. Even though they thought they were alone, they spoke quietly, making it hard to hear their conversation.

With a sigh, he sank onto the mossy ground. He would just have to wait until they moved on and continue to follow them. He looked forward to the end of this journey when he could put the whole thing to an end.

CHAPTER SEVEN

I**T WAS A** lie.

Errol kenned exactly where they needed to go next.

And what was there.

He hadn't been *there* in years, but the last time he had been, he remembered it clear as day.

A time when there was no truce between the MacLeods and the Harts. Though it was deep in MacLeod lands, the enemy was there. Watching through the trees.

Waiting.

Quietly.

Patiently.

When Errol's brother, Gavin, and the small party he was traveling with, stopped at the old graveyard to pay their respects to those long gone, they were ambushed.

Taken by surprise. All four men were cut down.

For no reason. They'd done naught wrong. Hadn't led any attacks. Hadn't hurt anyone.

When Gavin and his men hadn't returned, Laird MacLeod, he and Gavin's da, sent out a search party.

It was Errol who found his slain brother.

He closed his eyes and took a deep breath. The gruesome scene was forever emblazoned in his memory.

"Is something amiss?" Moira asked, placing a small hand on

his forearm. "Suddenly ye look unwell. Are ye suffering from the same affliction as Seema and the others?" Her voice was laced with concern.

But he paid no attention to that. Instead, he pulled his arm away, recoiling from her touch. The thought of his brother reminded him that Moira couldn't be trusted. That there was an underlying reason for this chase they were on.

He'd never been able to prove it, but he had always believed that the Harts were behind his brother's assassination.

"Did I do something wrong?" She asked when he didn't answer.

"Nay. Finish yer meal so we can return to the room. Ye need yer rest." He couldn't keep the gruffness out of his voice.

For a moment, Moira looked like she was going to put up a fight, but she snapped her mouth shut and after a moment, took a bite of stew.

They ate in silence and as they were finishing, she called over the serving wench to request a bowl of stew to bring with them.

"Seema's belly must be empty. She'll need sustenance."

Errol gave her a curt nod.

"Are ye for certs there is naught amiss?"

"E'erything is fine, Moira."

She sighed in resignation. "If ye insist." She popped the last bit of bread into her mouth and chewed. When she was done, she asked, "It will take us a day to get to the next location?"

"Aye."

"What do you think is there? Something of worth?"

Naught but bad memories. But he couldn't, wouldn't, tell her that. "I dinna ken. I suppose we'll find out on the morrow."

The serving wench arrived with their extra bowl of stew covered with a square of cloth.

Standing, Errol dropped enough coins on the table to cover the cost of their meals and escorted Moira to the door.

She walked slowly, taking care not to spill any of the stew as they made their way back to the inn and their room.

Seema sat at the window and smiled when they entered.

"We thought ye may be hungry, so we brought stew." Moira held up the bowl in her hand and approached Seema.

The maid put her hands up and shook her head. "I thank ye for the kind gesture, but I cannae accept."

Moira's face softened. She set the dish on the table and nodded. "I was hoping that ye would feel well enough to eat, but I see 'tis too early."

"Aye. My belly has settled some, but I dare no' eat just yet. Mayhap in the morn."

"We will head north in the morn, but if ye are still no' well, we will delay."

Seema shook her head. "Please, doonae stay for my sake. Ye need to continue on."

"And leave ye here alone? I think no'."

Errol watched the exchange betwixt the two women. Moira was genuinely concerned for the well-being of her maid. She sat near the woman, rubbing her hand along the maid's back in a comforting manner.

The journey ahead of them would not be an easy one. As he'd mentioned, it was a day's ride from their current location, however, it would take them much longer with Seema's current condition.

He remained silent. He would not be the one to tell Moira that he thought Seema should stay behind.

Moira patted Seema's hand. "We shall see how ye fare in the morn and decide then, aye?" She stood and looked at the bed and then to Errol, and then back to the bed. "Where are ye planning to sleep?"

"Dinnae fash, lass. The bed is ye and yer maid's. I will sleep on the floor."

She nodded her head in agreement. "That does appear to be our only option, doesnae it?"

He left the room to give the women their privacy as they readied themselves for bed.

When Moira called out to him to let him ken it was safe to enter, he looked to the bed and fought back a wave of disappointment in seeing that she was settled under the blankets already.

The thought was foreign to him. Why should he care that he didn't get a glimpse of her creamy skin? Her long hair cascading over her bare shoulders. The swell of her breasts. The roundness of her bottom.

Christ. He shook his head to clear it as he grabbed the extra blankets from the chair and laid them out on the floor. Then he snuffed out the candle, bathing them all in darkness.

He settled in for an uncomfortable night, but at least he wasn't sleeping outdoors on the cold ground. But then he would be able to look up at the night sky. See the stars shining above him. One of his favorite things to do.

Moira wasn't aught more than a mission. He didn't need to think about her in any way other than that. As a matter of fact, he would be smart not to do so. Especially if she was deceiving him.

"Sleep well, Errol." Moira said into the darkness and guilt overwhelmed him.

His thoughts were a mess. One minute he was certain she was leading him into a trap. The next he was thinking what it would feel like to taste her lips.

"Good night." He answered gruffly and closed his eyes, willing his mind to think of aught else other than the bonny lass lying in the bed just a few feet away from him.

ERROL WAS WIDE awake the next morn when he heard the women start to stir. He'd spent a restless night tossing and turning. The floor was hard under his back, but that wasn't what bothered him. He'd slept on much worse. Minus the beauty of being under the stars, the floor still beat sleeping on the ground.

But he couldn't get Moira out of his mind. All night long her visage was there every time he closed his eyes.

Moira's head popped over the side of the bed. "Good morn," she said in a sleepy voice as she rubbed her eyes.

Even with her messy hair and puffy eyes from sleep, she was still beautiful.

He nodded his head and stood. "I shall leave ye be so that ye can dress for the day. When ye are ready we can go break our fast."

He exited the room and waited in the hall while the women tended to their needs and dressed. It shouldn't take long. They hadn't packed much as they wanted to be light for the journey. Seema hadn't awakened during the night, and he took that as a good sign that whatever affliction she'd had hopefully passed.

"Errol, son of the MacLeod."

At his name, Errol turned. The man walking toward him looked familiar, but he couldn't put a name to the face. He appeared to be close to his father's age, and similar in stature.

"Richard Carlyle." The man introduced himself once he was near. "My wife and I are on our way to visit yer father at MacLeod Keep."

Errol recognized the name. Richard and his family were part of one of the unaffiliated clans that were scattered about the highlands.

"I am for certs my father will be happy to see ye both. How are yer sons?" If Errol recalled correctly, Richard had twin boys a few years younger than him.

Richard's eyes lit up at the mention of his children. "They are verra well, thank ye fer asking. They keep busy tending the cattle."

His wife joined him, and Richard draped an arm over her shoulder, pulling her closer. "Ye remember my wife, Caroline?"

Errol bowed to the woman. "'Tis lovely to see ye again, Lady Carlyle." The woman blushed and dipped her head.

The door opened and Moira stepped out into the hall, Seema

right behind her. "We are ready if ye are." She paused when she saw the Carlyles.

Errol cleared his throat. No doubt this run-in would be mentioned to his father when Richard arrived at MacLeod Keep. He would worry about dealing with his father later when he returned home. Hopefully with an arm full of riches.

"Richard, Caroline, may I introduce Moira and her maid, Seema."

Caroline stepped forward. "Good morn. Were ye on yer way to break yer fast? We are doing the same and would love for ye to join us." She turned to her husband. "Wouldnae we, Richard?"

"Och, aye," Richard said. He didn't appear to care one way or another.

Moira's gaze slid to Errol, her eyes round in question.

He shrugged. It didn't matter to him. Just as long as they finished quickly. They needed to get on the road.

Moira smiled. "We would love to."

The group made their way downstairs and into the dining hall where they were seated at a large table. Mugs of heather ale were served, followed by plates of smoked salmon, bannocks and porridge.

Moira ate heartily, but Errol noticed that Seema hadn't taken a single bite. Instead, her pallor was still off, as if she were ready to toss whatever contents were left in her belly. That didn't bode well for their travel plans.

"Are ye weel, Seema?" Moira asked, concern knitting her brows.

"Aye. Weel enough, I'd say. Though no' weel enough to eats still." She placed her hands on her stomach. "I fear 'tis still unsettled."

Caroline reached over and patted her hand. "Ye poor dear. Have ye been unweel?"

"Poor Seema has been dealing with a stomach affliction," Moira piped in. "We had hoped that she would feel better this morn." She smiled at Seema, patting her hand.

"I am sorry, Miss. I dinnae think I can continue on our journey. Mayhap I should stay here and await ye on yer return to MacLeod Keep?"

Moira shook her head. "I cannae leave ye here. We will stay until ye have recovered." She said matter-of-factly and pierced Errol with a fierce look. "Right?"

He sighed, but reluctantly agreed. They couldn't leave her here to fend for herself. There was no other choice to be made.

"MacLeod Keep, ye say?" Caroline interjected. "We are headed there ourselves and we have room. We would be glad to return ye home."

None of them spoke up to say that MacLeod Keep wasn't Seema's home. But Anna and Fina were there. They would no doubt welcome her in their circle.

"We cannae accept such a kind offer," Moira spoke. "But—"

"That is verra generous of ye. I will gladly accept if the offer still stands," Seema said quietly.

Caroline beamed happily. "Of course, child."

The rest of the meal went quickly. Errol and Richard spoke about the journey and he ensured the man that he would be rewarded generously for his kind offer.

His father would not be happy to find out that their original party of six was now a party of two. He would deal with those ramifications at a later date.

Two hours later, Moira and Seema said their tearful goodbyes and Moira waited until the Carlyles and Seema were out of sight afore turning to him.

"It seems 'tis just us now."

Was that wariness cracking her voice?

"Aye. We should get moving." He picked up her satchel and moved to their waiting horses. Securing Moira's bag on her mare, he turned to find her standing in the same spot. "Lass, we need to leave." His urgency to be on their way had him sounding gruff even to his own ears.

"Has anyone e'er told ye that ye are grumpier than a mutt

stung by a bee?" She mumbled as she shuffled over.

Helping her mount, he made sure she was settled afore mounting his own horse. "In not as many words, aye." He finally said and chuckled as he kicked his horse into a slow walk, waiting for Moira to catch up.

"How long will it take to get to our destination?"

"If we hurry we can make it by late afternoon." That was a lofty goal. The ride would take them the better part of the day. The coming night they would have to sleep under the stars.

She prodded her horse into a trot, and he followed suit.

"Do you really think at one time our clans were united by marriage?" Moira asked.

"Nay."

"'Twould be something if it were true, would in no'?"

"Aye. 'Twould be most unexpected."

"Ye're for certs ye ken where we are going?"

Errol closed his eyes and said a silent prayer for patience. It would be a very long day if the lass didn't cease her rambling. He preferred traveling with his warriors. They didn't feel the need to fill the silence with incessant chatter.

"Errol?"

"What, Moira?"

"Ye didnae answer me."

He sighed, feeling as if the world was weighing his shoulders down. "I ken the area verra well." He wouldn't tell her why. Some things needed to remain secret—especially if her family was behind his brother's death.

She smiled. "See? 'Twas no' so hard to answer."

He rolled his eyes and shook his head. It was going to be a long ride.

"I hope Anna, Fina, and Seema will feel better soon. 'Tis odd that they fell ill, is it no'?"

When he didn't answer, she kept talking and answering her own questions. "And that we havenae."

And that was how they rode for the next few hours. While

she yammered on constantly, he was trying to listen to their surroundings. Not an easy task since it appeared the lass didn't ken how to be quiet. Danger could be lurking in the shadows.

Moira may be a Hart and leading him into an ambush, but at this time, she was still his ward, and he would ensure her safety.

"Are ye listening? I feel like ye are ignoring me."

"I am no' ignoring ye."

"Ye arenae listening to me, though."

Errol stiffened as he heard a twig crack.

He looked at Moira and put his index finger to his lips, signaling her to be quiet.

At first, she looked confused and then she must have understood because her eyes grew round as platters. She moved to look around, but he called her name so she would keep her attention on him.

He was almost positive they were being followed. He didn't want their stalkers to ken he was aware of their presence. Slowly, he moved his hand to his sword and rested his palm on the hilt, ready to withdraw it.

Moira's eyes tracked his movements, and she leaned forward, feigning that she was petting her mare, and pulled a dagger from her boot and hid it up her sleeve.

For the first time since they'd left, he longed to hear her rambling.

Looking ahead they were approaching a line of trees with low-hanging branches. It made the area dark. If there was a perfect place for them to be attacked, that was it.

He looked at Moira, whispered for her to be on guard. "Remain calm, lass," he said quietly.

As they entered the darkness, all was quiet. No birds chirping. There was naught. Errol masked his face into a relaxed position, but his body was wound tight, ready to strike.

Halfway through the branch tunnel, they attacked. A man ran from the cover of the trees, sword raised high in the air, as he let out a cry.

Errol jumped from his horse and quickly sliced the man down. He fell in a thud at Errol's feet. His horse angrily stomped the ground, nostrils flaring.

Moira screamed, her booted foot kicking out and catching one of the attackers square on the chin. He stumbled back but regained his balance quickly. Errol ran over and the man spun at his approach, sword out ready to fight.

"Errol! Behind ye!" Moira yelled and he ducked just in time. He heard the hiss of the blade whisk over his head.

He kicked out his right leg and knocked the man off balance. As he did, the attacker in front of him swung and Errol felt the sting of his blade cut his upper arm. Ignoring the searing pain, he blocked the next swing with his sword and gave a shove, pushing the man back. He thrust his sword and the man leapt out of reach. They parried back and forth.

Moira's yell filled his ears, and he whipped his head around to find her. She was on the ground, running, being chased by another bandit. Errol's blood boiled. His rage building, he spun, swinging his sword. Smiling as he felt his blade sink into soft flesh, catching on bone. Blood gushed, and he kicked the man off his blade.

He ran in Moira's direction. Pulling his dagger from his boot, he thought about throwing it at the heathen who chased her, but it was too risky. If he missed and hit her, he would never forgive himself.

Catching up to the two, he threw his body at the man in a full-on tackle. The man fell to the ground under him with an 'oof' as his breath left him.

He picked up the man by his tunic, bringing his face close to his. "Who are ye?" Errol growled. "How many of ye are there?"

The man was grabbing at his chest, unable to breathe.

Errol's eyes clashed with Moira's. "Are ye hurt?"

She shook her head, her eyes wide and terrified.

"'Tis okay, lass. Sit. Breathe." She dropped onto the ground and hugged her knees to her chest. A tear ran down her cheek.

There would be time to comfort her later. First, he needed to find out how many attackers there were. Who they were and what they wanted?

He shook the man. "How many?" He spat, fury running through his veins.

"F-f-four," the man sputtered.

Errol had already killed three. "Including ye, or other than ye?"

"I-including me." The man wheezed as he tried to control his breathing.

Errol pushed him away.

The man scrambled to his hands and knees, sputtering and coughing.

Checking on Moira, Errol knelt beside her. "Are ye for certs ye arenae hurt?"

She nodded, her hand reaching out to the slash on his arm. "Ye're hurt though. Ye'll need to be stitched."

"I am fine. I've suffered worse." He walked over to the man hunched on all fours and kicked him in the stomach, making the man fall to his back. He rolled to his side, clutching his middle.

Errol would break every one of his ribs. Every bone in his body. He would do whatever he had to get the answers he sought.

"What are ye after? Who sent ye?"

"Y-y-ye seek treasure."

"That is what ye attacked us for? Bloody bastards." Errol kicked him again and the man howled. "Are ye trying to make the MacLeod an enemy of ye?"

The man spat blood and Errol took a sick satisfaction in seeing the red stain the ground. "We dinnae care that ye are a MacLeod. Or that ye are with a Hart bitch," he snarled.

Errol was on him quickly, smashing his fists into the man's face. Over and over. He felt the bones crunch under his assault. And he reveled in the feeling. His rage out of control. The realization that the bastard could have killed Moira.

Moira.

He heard her screams. Her pleas to cease.

His breath ragged, he stopped and sank back on his heels, cradling his head in his blood-covered hands.

Their attacker's face was a mass of tissue and bone. And blood. Lots of it.

He had called Moira a bitch. More than aught, that was what spurred him on.

Moira approached him cautiously and he hated the fear he saw in her eyes.

"I would ne'er hurt ye, lass," he confessed. He blew out a long breath as he flexed his fingers, his knuckles bruised and swollen.

She nodded. "I ken," she said quietly. "Let me tend to yer wounds?"

"Nay, no' now." He looked at the carnage around them. "We need to move in case others are following them. I need to get ye to safety."

"Can ye ride?"

He smiled. "I've ridden with worse. Let us go."

CHAPTER EIGHT

THE BOTHY THEY came across appeared to have not been visited for quite some time. A thick layer of dust covered the sparse furniture, but there was dry wood stacked near the fireplace that they could use for a fire.

After helping Errol into a chair, she placed the logs in the fire, thankful they were there and that she wouldn't have to waste time collecting wood. Once she had the fire started, she moved to the one bed in the small space. The throws were old, but they would do. She pulled them off the bed and brought them outside to shake them out.

She kenned she should do the same to the mattress, but there wasn't any time. Errol had been bleeding quite heavily since he was first cut, and the bleeding got worse the longer they rode. She was scared that he wouldn't be able to stay astride his horse if they had to ride much longer.

After she remade the bed, ensuring to put one of the throws down for Errol to lay on, she helped him to the bed.

He laid down with a grunt, a wince distorting his face.

Moira was certain he was hurt even more than he was telling her.

They needed clean water but didn't have any other than the filled skins they carried. They would have to do for now. She would look for fresh water after she took care of Errol.

She looked around the bothy to see what type of supplies had been left behind, hoping there were items of use for their situation. She found a stack of folded linens, and pulled a couple from the middle and shook them out. Since they were covered for the most part by the linens surrounding them, they were the cleanest of the bunch.

From her satchel she pulled out a needle and thread. Thankful to Seema for handing them to her afore they parted.

"Just in case," she had said with a sad smile.

Moira thought she was being silly.

Until now.

She shivered at the thought of how much danger they were in. Afore they were attacked, Moira saw their journey as an adventure. Danger never crossed her mind.

Now she realized how wrong she'd been.

Looking through the cupboard, she found a few bottles of ale. Not kenning how long they'd been here, she wouldn't drink them, but she could use them to clean Errol's wounds. She grabbed one and after dragging a small table near the bed, she placed all the items she'd gathered atop it.

Errol caught her hand. "Lass, I will be fine. I just need to rest a bit."

He reminded her of Seema. She'd uttered those exact words at the inn.

"I agree, ye will be fine. Howe'er ye still need stitches, though I must warn ye. At home, sewing was no' an interest of mine, so these may no' be pretty, but they will staunch the bleeding to be sure."

He gave her a small smile. "I am no' the least bit surprised that ye found no interest in sewing."

"Watch it," she warned. "I may be tempted to punch ye in yer arm for yer teasing."

"Duly noted. In my bag is a skin of ale, can ye get it? I think I'd like a swallow afore ye start."

She did as he asked and handed him the skin. With a grunt, he pulled himself into a sitting position and took a long pull. After he was done, he met her eyes.

"I'm ready," he said, lying back in the bed.

Cutting away the remnants of his bloody sleeve, she revealed the wound. It was deep but the slice was clean.

"This may burn," she warned as she poured the ale on the cut.

Errol hissed through his clenched teeth but said naught and remained still.

Moira was thankful it wasn't a jagged cut. Her sewing skills were not aught to be proud of. But with no other choice available she set to work threading the needle, and afore starting, she said, "I apologize."

His eyes clashed with hers. "Dinnae. I am thankful for yer assistance."

Biting her lip, she wiped away the blood as best as she could, then pierced his flesh with the needle, drawing it through to the other side. She couldn't help but cringe each time she repeated the action.

Errol watched her with a pained expression but said naught.

She began to hum. An old tune her mother used to sing to her when she was a wee lass. She didn't ken why, but it released some of the tension filling the room. Even Errol, for all that he was going through, seemed to relax a bit, which made the process easier.

His eyes never stopped watching her. She tried to ignore his gaze. Ignore the heat that blossomed in her belly. But it was hard. Even as she concentrated on the task at hand. Thankfully, her stitches held and by the time she finished, the flow of blood had stopped.

"Ye did good, lass."

With a small smile playing on her lips, she began to wrap his arm in clean linen. "Ye may no' thank me once ye see the scar left behind."

He chuckled. "It will join all my others."

She frowned at that. For some unkenned reason, the thought of him having so many scars bothered her. Though it shouldn't.

He was a fierce warrior. Had fought alongside his family, just as her own brother, Alpin, had with hers. If she were to guess, she was certain they could compare battle scars and come out even.

"Ye should probably rest. Ye lost a large amount of blood."

Errol sat up in the bed, picked up the skin of ale she'd placed there, and took a long swallow. Gingerly, he rotated his shoulder, testing the limits of how much movement he still had.

Other than dealing with the pain of the cut, he still had full use of his arm. The wound wasn't near enough his shoulder to cause issue there.

Outside, the birds had ceased their singsong. It was getting later in the day. She assumed they were hiding in their nests to wait until the morn. She looked warily at the door. She'd bolted it shut, but if someone had wanted to enter, they wouldn't have much of a problem. The bothy provided shelter. But it was old. Weathered.

"Dinnae fash. We are safe."

Moira studied Errol's face. "How can ye be sure?"

"The men that ambushed us were working alone. More than likely they heard us speak of what we were doing at the pub last eve."

That made sense.

"They wouldnae have told many more people. The more people, the smaller the cut."

She worried her bottom lip as she thought about the different things that could happen to them. "What if someone realizes they are missing and comes looking for them?"

Errol shook his head. "Nay. I dinnae see that happening. This is the safest place for us tonight. In the morn, we can finish our journey to the next stop."

Looking around she kenned he was right. It didn't make sense to travel this late in the day.

Her stomach growled, echoing in the empty cabin.

"I'm sorry," she said as she laid her palm on her stomach. "I fear the meal we ate at the inn this morn is long gone."

"Are ye for certs 'tis just hunger and no' the same affliction that has dropped the others?"

"Aye. I feel fine."

Errol pushed off the bed and stood beside her.

In doing so she was reminded of just how very tall he was. He towered over her slight frame, and she had to crane her neck to look up and meet his eyes. Eyes that watched her softly. He lifted his hand as if he was going to touch her face, but he paused mid-air. For a few moments his hand hovered there before he masked his expression and dropped it to his side.

She took a deep breath. For the briefest of moments, she wondered what it would feel like for Errol to caress her cheek. What was she thinking?

"Ye shouldnae be standing." She said to focus her thoughts on something else other than the handsome warrior standing afore her. Placing her palms on his chest she gave him a gentle nudge toward the bed. He didn't budge, but heat warmed her palms, moving up her arms to stain her cheeks with a blush, she was certain of it.

She snapped her hands back as if she were burned.

His face softened again, but his eyes burned into her. Had he felt that same heat?

Then he looked away and whatever had passed betwixt them was gone.

Moving around her, he picked up his sword, and tucked his dagger into his boot.

"Where are ye going?"

"We need to sup and there is naught here to stave off our hunger."

"But yer arm…"

"'Twill be fine. 'Tis no longer bleeding thanks to ye. 'Twillnae take long. Mayhap get a pot ready?"

She nodded. Then thought of something. "But wait. We

dinnae have water."

He paused, his hand on the door latch after he'd lifted the bolt of wood that secured the door. "There has to be a well around here. I will look for that first. Stay inside, lass," he ordered quietly. "Please, for once, listen to me." When his eyes met hers, they were soft with his plea.

Wetting her dry lips with her tongue, she nodded. Adding more things for him to fash about would do neither of them any good, so she would do as she'd been told.

He disappeared outside, closing the door behind him. The interior of the bothy, though small, felt huge without Errol there to fill the space. She rubbed her hands up and down her arms. Even with the fire burning bright, she suddenly felt chilled. His heat had warmed the room.

As she tried to gather her thoughts, the realization of what they had gone through earlier finally settled over her.

They'd been attacked.

They could have been killed.

And for what? For something that so far alluded to a secret love pact between the MacLeods and the Harts.

Sighing, she forced herself to move. Keeping her body busy would keep her mind from focusing on what they'd endured earlier.

On a low shelf, Moira found a large pot that they could use to cook whatever it was that Errol managed to catch. The fire burned bright, and she now noticed the spit that had been hung from one side of the fireplace to the other.

The door opened and Moira spun with a small squeal.

"'Tis just me, lass," Errol announced. In his hands was a bucket.

"Fresh water?"

"Aye." He placed it on the table and turned to the door again. "No one is about. 'Tis only us in the area. Ye neednae fash so."

She hadn't realized that she had her palm clutched over her heart. Words escaped her and even if they would come, she didn't trust her voice. Her heart was beating frantically. So, she only nodded.

Errol ducked back outside and she let out a slow, steadying breath. Being in the bothy was much better than sleeping outside, open to all the elements, including more bandits that could be tracking them. Aye, Errol said there weren't any more. But she didn't trust a word of what that louse had said before Errol silenced him forever with his fists. Would he really admit if there were others that were going to follow behind?

Nay, she didn't think so.

Opening the door to the one cupboard near what she believed was a prep table, she was surprised to see several corked pots. Picking up one, she tugged on the cork. It had been sealed snuggly and took her a couple of tries to remove it. Once she did, she smiled. The spicy scent of pepper assaulted her nose. Were all of these spices? If so, she was fairly confident she would be able to season whatever meat Errol was able to find.

A cook she was not. Nor did she have any ambition to be one, but she'd watched Oona prepare enough meats to ken that the answer to an edible meal was the spices one added.

By the time Errol returned, she had managed to open all the pots.

"A single hare, but 'twill get us fed and provide sustenance enough until the morrow." He grinned sheepishly, the look completely transforming his features. "I dressed it for ye. For some reason, I thought that wasnae aught ye were familiar with."

Placing her hands on her hips, she tried to school her face into a serious look, but judging by Errol's laughter, she failed. Huffing out a breath, she approached and took the carcass from him. "Ye are correct. My da wouldnae be proud."

At the mention of her father, his brows drew together. "Aye, well, ye were verra handy with the needle and thread. I'll be sure to convince yer da of that if he doesnae strike me down first once he learns that we are traipsing about in the highlands alone."

She waved her hands in the air in dismissal. "Pfft. Ye returning me home safely will garner his thanks and naught more."

He grunted.

Moira didn't think Errol believed her, but it was the truth. Her da was kenned as a fierce warrior, and he was, but he was also right and just. His moves were well thought out. Having Moira return home in one piece, hopefully, with a treasure as well, would be all her father needed.

CHAPTER NINE

Errol had to give Moira credit. She held her father in high respect. Which, as his daughter, she should, but Moira didn't ken her father like he did. She didn't see the same side of him that he saw. The warrior side.

The enemy side.

He'd met Laird Arthur Hart on more than one occasion. The man was as fierce as Errol's own father. He actually believed the men were similar in personalities and that was why they could never come to any reasonable agreement. Neither wanted to give in to the other's demands.

And Errol couldn't blame them.

There was a lot at stake considering the land and holdings betwixt the two clans. Neither side was going to roll over and let the other seize what they believed was rightfully theirs.

The smell of roasted hare wafted over to him. He wasn't sure what Moira had done to the meat, but the scent was divine and his stomach growled in response. Or mayhap he was just starving since he hadn't supped since this morn.

The sun had gone down and they were enveloped in darkness. He found torches and lit them to brighten the bothy, bathing it in warm golden light.

"'Tis ready, I believe." She blushed. "Please be kind. I have ne'er cooked aught afore."

"It seems ye are having a lot of firsts this trip," he quipped. "E'en if ye havenae, I wouldnae be aught but kind. And thankful." He helped her with the spit and slid the roasted hare onto the prep table.

"Thank ye."

He raised a brow in question.

Moira pointed to the hare. "For this. For the water. I dinnae think I have given ye my thanks yet. And most of all for this adventure. I ken ye didnae want to accompany me," she scoffed and pointed to his arm. "And look where that got us. Look where it got ye. With a sliced arm that we can only hope doesnae fester while we are so far from help."

He lifted his arm and looked at the bandage covering his wound. "I had a verra good healer. I am for certs 'twillnae fester." He spoke the truth. He didn't understand why it mattered. Why he cared that he put Moira at ease. Why he felt the need to compliment her.

But he did.

Moira dipped her head but not afore he saw the blush that splashed her cheeks pink.

They ate in silence except for when he praised her for the delicious hare she'd prepared. Once again, she'd blushed, but didn't hide her face this time.

After the meal, Errol made another trip to the well and fetched fresh water to get them through the night. Outside the night was still, not even a breeze to sway the branches. An owl hooting in the distance the only noise. He believed the four men that had ambushed them were the only ones that had tracked them. He'd seen no signs of anyone else. Even so, he'd sleep with his sword at his side and his dagger under his pillow this night.

He entered the bothy and set the bucket of water on the prep table as Moira bolted the door behind him.

"We should get some rest. The hour is growing late."

Moira nodded. "Ye especially. Ye need to sleep to help ye heal." She said in an almost motherly tone as her eyes fell on the bed.

The *only* bed.

A situation they had found themselves in afore. But Seema was with them then. Now, it was just the two of them.

Alone.

In a bothy deep in the highlands.

"I will sleep on the floor," he said, hoping to ease her wariness.

"Ye will do no such thing. Ye willnae get a restful sleep on the floor." She eyed the bed again, biting her lip. "'Tis large enough for us both." She approached the bed and looked it over, nodding. "Aye. If I lay on this side near the edge we willnae touch."

He closed his eyes and blew out a breath. Not a good idea. Errol didn't think that he would get a minute of sleep kenning that Moira lay so close that he would be able to feel the warmth emanating off her body. So close that he only needed to reach out his hand to be able to touch her. He wouldn't, of course.

But he would spend the whole night fighting off the temptation.

Nay. He couldn't. "I dinnae believe that is a good idea."

Moira raised her eyebrows. "Well, I guess 'tis a good thing I am no' asking ye, then, isnae it?" She sighed, rubbing her forehead. "'Tis been a long, trying day. We dinnae ken what the morrow brings. Because of that, the bed is needed for us both." She crossed her arms as if daring him to challenge her.

A spitfire.

Errol appreciated that. He could understand why his sister and Moira got on so well. Anna also kenned what she wanted and went after it head first without thinking of the consequences. A sure-fire way to get into trouble, but since she usually remained at MacLeod Keep it wasn't an issue.

Moira seemed to possess the same headstrong attitude.

"I will sleep on top of the throws."

She tilted her head to the side. "Will ye no' be cold?"

"Nay. I've my plaid to keep me warm. I'll have easier access to my sword that way as well." Her eyes rounded as she looked around the bothy, her eyes pausing on the window. "Do ye think we will be attacked again?"

He shook his head. "There is no one about. But 'tis best to stay vigilant always."

Nodding, she rubbed her hands up and down her arms.

"Get ready for bed. All will be well," Errol promised.

He moved to another part of the bothy to give her privacy and when they finally settled into bed, with Moira under the throws, and Errol on top of them, he could do naught but stare at the shadows of the fire that still burned bright, dancing across the ceiling. The only light since he'd snuffed the torches afore lying down.

His arm was sore and felt stiff. He tried to stretch it out without causing too much movement on the bed, so he didn't disturb Moira. He also took care not to open the stitches that Moira had meticulously sewn.

"Errol?" Moira whispered after quite some time had passed. "Are ye awake?"

Her voice was low enough that if he were asleep he wouldn't have heard her. He could pretend that he hadn't. But why do that? He wasn't sleeping either. Besides, she had his curiosity piqued. Why did she call for him?

"Aye?" He answered.

"Why do you think our families hate each other?"

He sighed, the sound so loud in the space of the small bothy it seemed to vibrate off the walls. "'Tis no' an easy answer. And one ye shouldnae fash about."

"Why no'? Why do men always say that women mustnae concern themselves with such things?" She rolled to her side and met his gaze, her expression serious. "We are always verra much affected by the actions taken by men. 'Tis only natural that we ask about it. That we want to ken."

Errol pushed himself up to a sitting position and Moira did the same as she watched and waited patiently for him to answer.

"I think sometimes men who carry the weight of the world

on their shoulders think they can protect the women they love by no' discussing the ugliness of war."

She chewed on her lower lip as she thought about what he'd said.

"But dinnae those same men ken that a strong woman by their side could help ease their burden?"

He cocked his head to the side as he looked at Moira. Truly looked at her. Not as his younger sister's best friend, but as a woman who had more than likely, on numerous occasions, been told to leave when serious matters came up in conversation.

Her argument had merit.

"I believe ye are correct. There is validity to the point in which ye have made."

She smiled sweetly. Not a cocky smile as if she kenned she were right. But one where she seemed happy that he'd taken her words into consideration. Surely, with all her siblings, and she being the eldest daughter, her words were taken seriously to some extent. Not when it came to war and fighting, but for certs in other aspects of whatever it was that women did to occupy their days.

"Ye answered one of my questions. But no' the most important one. What has happened betwixt our families to cause such long and unforgiving rifts?"

He closed his eyes and leaned his head against the wall, blowing out a slow breath as the vision of his brother's broken and dead body lying on the ground flooded his mind.

"I ken no' what caused the hatred all those years ago. I only ken what I have experienced myself."

Her brows drew together. "I dinnae understand." She shifted closer to him.

Errol should pull away. Put that distance betwixt them, but he didn't. Instead, he let the heat from her body warm his arm that was so close to touching her.

"Did my family hurt ye?" Her eyes traveled the length of his body as if she were searching for wounds or scars branded with the Hart name.

"Aye. Nay." He blew out an exasperated breath and raked his fingernails over his scalp. "My brother. He was on a watch with other guards from our clan. They were on MacLeod lands. No' raiding. They had done naught wrong."

Moira's hand flew to her mouth, her face stricken as if she kenned what his next words were going to be.

"The whole party was struck down. On our own lands," he spat. "'Twas the Harts," he said matter-offactly, his voice dripping with disdain.

"Nay," Moira gasped. "We wouldnae. Why? If they werenae on Hart land, but e'en then, they wouldnae have been killed for it." She shook her head vehemently. "Nay. Ye are wrong."

"I am no'," he growled, and she shrank back from the vehemence in his voice. "My brother was only ten and seven."

"Errol," she whispered. "I am so sorry. But my, we, we wouldnae have done such an atrocity." She reached for his arm, but he pulled away.

He didn't want her touch. Her pity.

He wanted her to admit to what her family had done to destroy his.

She clenched the hand that still hung in the air into a tiny fist afore bringing it to her chest.

"I refuse to believe that. My clan is one of peace. We only use violence when 'tis forced upon us."

Errol barked out a laugh. The sound echoing off the walls of the bothy. "So naive. Dinnae ye ken? Just as the MacLeods have done our fair share of misdeeds, so have the Harts. Neither of us are innocent. Why dinnae ye think there is no peace betwixt our clans? My brother's death is one of the reasons. Until we see justice for Gavin, we will no' rest."

He pushed off the bed, ignoring the pain that lanced through his arm at the sudden movement.

"Errol," she called.

He spun and shook his head. "Nay. I dinnae want to speak of

it any longer." His arm hurt. His head hurt, and most of all, his heart hurt. He hadn't wanted to bring up Gavin. Didn't really ken why he did. For one weak moment, he opened up to his enemy. Because that was what Moira Hart was—his enemy.

Aye, he'd help her on this silly quest of hers. But he wouldn't open his heart up to her again. He'd shown her his weakness, and she could use that against him. He'd been a fool.

He dropped into the chair in front of the fire and rested his sword against the arm. Distance from Moira was what he needed. When she was close, he couldn't think straight. His thoughts jumbled as if they were being tossed around in the river and then dropping over the falls.

It wouldn't happen again.

"Go to sleep," he murmured.

Moira opened her mouth and he thought she was going to fight him on it. But he pierced her with a glare, and she shrunk back, sliding down the bed and brought the throws up to her chin. He really hadn't meant to scare the lass. But he needed to show her that they weren't friends. They never would be.

He turned to the dancing flames of the fire. His gaze followed the bursts of sparks made when a log collapsed, sending embers in all directions.

His thoughts were like those sparks. Roaming around carelessly with no sense of direction.

It was a position he hadn't been faced with afore.

And he found he didn't like it one bit.

THE TWO HAD finally settled into bed for the night. Well, the lass was in bed. The MacLeod sat in front of the fire, staring into the dancing flames, a dour look settled on his face.

He was lucky that he hadn't been caught up in the battle that had ensued earlier. He easily could have been. As it was, it was a miracle that his presence hadn't been noticed.

The four men that had attacked the MacLeod and the Hart bitch had met a quick death at the end of the MacLeod's blade. Hell, even the Hart bitch had a dagger with which she fought. Not that she needed it. The MacLeod was well-trained and even though he fought four men, they were no match for him.

Once again, he'd remained in the shadows. Watching quietly. Intently.

He needed to learn the MacLeod's fighting preferences. What threw him off. The weaknesses he tried to hide.

All of those would prove to be beneficial when it was his time to cut the warrior down.

He wasn't worried about the Hart wench. Her little dagger didn't frighten him. However, the MacLeod kenned how to fight. He had spent his whole life in preparation. Training. Honing his skills.

Anger filled him at the thought. His own father had never taken the time to ensure he got his training. Nay, instead his father tried to pass him off to the maids.

"I have nay use for a crippled imbecile," he would tell them, never looking him in the eye. Barely acknowledging him. The only time his father paid him any attention was to speak about how much of a disappointment he was.

He sniffed and swiped at his eyes. He hated how his father made him feel. Even now, when he'd been dead for years.

The vice-like grip he held on him was suffocating. Stealing all breath from his lungs.

With no need to watch the window any longer, he went to his bag and pulled out his plaid, wrapping it around his shoulders. It would be preferable to sleep near a fire this night, but he couldn't risk anyone seeing the flame.

Moving into the woods, he found shelter under a low hanging pine and settled onto a bed of needles for the night.

He would be ready to move tomorrow when they emerged. Until then, he would get a few hours of rest.

"See, father," he said, eyes looking up to the starry night sky. "I can do this. Ye couldnae, but I will succeed where ye failed. Take my word for it."

◆━━━━━◆▸

CHAPTER TEN

MOIRA LAY IN bed, her head ducked low so that she was buried under the throws. Was what Errol had said true? He was fierce and sorrowful at the same time while he had told her what had happened to his brother. She couldn't see her clan acting in such a manner without just cause.

But somebody had.

Ten and seven. The same age as her youngest sister, Morven.

So young to suffer such a fate.

Errol had loved his brother very much. She could see it shining in the hurt of his eyes as he relayed the story. He'd spared her the details, but she could only imagine how horrific it had been. Her clan had suffered losses as well. But unlike Errol, her family was whole. She couldn't imagine the pain of losing one of her siblings. Aye, they annoyed her nearly every day, but she wouldn't have it any other way. Her life would be empty without one of them in it, poking into her business. Teasing her for always being locked away in the annals room. Her older brothers tugging on her hair as they walked by.

Of course, she had kenned from Anna that their brother had died, but never once had she told Moira how, so she had always assumed it was a tragic accident.

She wondered if Anna kenned how Gavin had really died? Or if that was another secret to be kept from her because she was a female.

For a few long moments, Moira watched Errol's silhouette, outlined by the light of the fire. His shoulders were slumped forward, and his chin dipped down. More than likely he was caught up in painful memories that he'd rather soon forget. But she saw his vulnerability.

Errol MacLeod loved those around him deeply. She was unsure what the morrow would bring. How they would get along and she wanted to kick herself for stirring up all the hurtful memories. She had thought the question was innocent enough. Something to get them talking.

How wrong she had been.

With a sigh, she turned to face the wall, her back to Errol, feeling ashamed of what she'd done—even if it was unintentional. She could only hope in the morning he would still be willing to escort her on this adventure.

But she would also understand if he refused and demanded they return home.

After all, how could they get around his thought that her family had killed a member of his? She didn't think they could.

When Moira woke the next morning the chair where Errol had moved to was empty. She sat up, rubbing the sleep from her eyes and scanned the interior of the bothy. The fire burned low from lack of attention and a shiver vibrated through her body at the chill in the air.

Errol was nowhere to be found. Her heart picked up speed. Had he abandoned her? Nay, he wouldn't have.

Would he? Mayhap. She had clearly upset him the night afore.

Insecurity turned her stomach as she thought about being alone here. Far from Hartsmoor. Deep in MacLeod lands and with people out there kenning that she and Errol were searching for some sort of treasure. It would not bode well for her. What would she do if bandits attacked like they had the day afore? She only had her dagger for protection.

The small blade would mayhap give her some time, but if

there was more than one attacker, she would be disarmed very quickly.

She dressed with haste and washed her face with some of the water from the bucket that still sat on the prep table. Noticing Errol's travel bag by the door, Moira breathed a sigh of relief.

He hadn't left her.

But where was he?

The door swung open, and Errol grunted a 'good morn' as he brushed past her.

Her fist clutched at her chest, trying to tame the erratic beat of her heart. He'd frightened her when he'd entered.

"I am glad to see ye've awakened. We should go," Errol said, his voice devoid of any emotion.

That was it. There was none of the softness to his voice that she'd seen glimpses of the previous day. Of course, that was afore the events of the night had happened. The reveal of his true hatred for the Harts.

Moira straightened her shoulders. She wouldn't let Errol ken that he got under her skin.

"The horses are ready," he stated gruffly as he bent and grabbed his bag.

"As am I." Moira stated. If he was going to talk in short bursts, so could she. She picked up her bag and when she passed him, he snatched it from her hands to carry it out to be tied to her horse. She bit the inside of her cheek to keep from smiling.

It appeared that no matter how angry Errol was, his manners were still intact.

The sky was gray, filled with clouds that Moira was certain would cry rain upon them soon. Early morning mist covered the mountains as they rode in silence, making their way through thick trees and rocky hillsides. The ride was treacherous and a few times, they had to stop to give the horses a respite. The rest also gave Moira's heart time to slow its frightfully fast beating. She felt on edge.

Whenever she stole a glance at Errol, he sat with his back

ramrod straight, eyes searching their surroundings, but never landing on her, her unease lifted a bit. He watched vigilantly for aught that might be amiss.

Kenning that he was taking such care for her safety was heartwarming, but cool at the same time. Since last night, he'd erected walls that she couldn't seem to penetrate.

But words had been few as Errol finally slowed to a stop and she urged her horse to do the same.

It was then that she looked where they'd stopped.

A kirkyard. A shiver ran down her back at the realization. It was old. The headstones lilted in all directions. Some had been overtaken with dark green moss and she could no longer see the name engraved in the stone.

Errol dismounted and Moira frowned.

"W-what are we doing here?" She looked around nervously, feeling uncomfortable.

"'Tis the next stop on yer map."

Once again her pulse quickened. "A kirkyard? Why? I've no interest in disturbing those at rest."

But Errol wasn't paying her any attention. Instead, his eyes were focused on a spot near one of the tipped headstones. His head dropped, shoulders slumping forward.

"Errol?" She called out to him, but he didn't answer.

Sliding off her horse, she slowly approached. He looked distraught, his handsome features distorted with pain.

She reached out her hand, her palm on his arm. "Errol?" She asked again. Something wasn't right.

He pulled away with a hiss as if her hand touching him burnt his flesh.

"What is wrong?" She asked quietly, retracting her hand. Kenning that something was bothering him, but she didn't ken what.

"This is where it happened," Errol finally spoke, his voice low.

He didn't have to explain to her what he was referring to. His brother. What cruel game was fate playing with them that the map would lead them to the site of his brother's death? If aught, Errol now had more reason to hate her than afore.

"I am sorry." The words felt bitter on her tongue. Insignificant in the heavy moment where Errol was lost in memories from that time.

Walking away, Moira allowed Errol time to spend with the memory of his brother. She sat down under a large tree and watched his throat bob as he swallowed down his emotions. Minutes passed but she would not complain or tell him to hurry along and stop whatever he was doing.

Because he was grieving.

And she wouldn't interrupt that.

As he worked through what he needed to, Moira pushed off the ground. The spring sun was warm as she tipped her face upward, letting the rays warm her cheeks. The rain that had threatened earlier had dissipated leaving beautiful weather in its wake. Nearby colorful flowers littered the ground. Picking a handful, she gathered them and wove discarded stems together, then wound the braid around the stems of the flowers she'd picked, creating a colorful, fragrant bouquet.

Carefully, she approached Errol. His face had softened a bit from earlier and when she approached he didn't scowl at her.

Kneeling at his feet, she placed the bouquet on the ground near his boots and said a quick prayer before moving to stand beside Errol.

"I ken ye doonae believe me," she said softly. "But I really am sorry. No one should have to suffer the loss of a sibling. Gavin seems that he was loved verra much."

Moira could see the flexing of Errol's jaw as he clenched his teeth.

"I've said my peace," he said and spun on his heel to walk toward his horse who was grazing on the dewy grass. From his travel bag, he pulled the skin with ale and took a long swig. "Does yer map say what we are looking for here?"

The sudden change of conversation showed that Errol didn't want to speak of his brother any longer.

With a sigh, she pulled out the map and unfurled it, studying the pictures that she could retain from memory at this point. Like the other stop at the chapel, the map said naught about what they were looking for. She shook her head.

Nodding in annoyance, he rolled his lips inward. "Great," he mumbled. "I suppose we are to hope that luck is on our side and whate'er is here just presents itself."

Moira chewed at her fingernail, considering his words. He wasn't wrong. While the map gave a minimal visual of the areas they needed to go to, hints to what they needed to find were nonexistent.

Walking along the headstones, she tried to read some of the names. Some she couldn't but others she could. Moss, algae, and stone worn smooth from the weather made reading some of the names, dates and remarks difficult. Not surprising the MacLeod name was prominent. "How old is this kirkyard? Do ye ken?"

"I dinnae. 'Tis been here for as long as I can remember and long afore then."

One of the headstones caught her attention. There was what looked to be a symbol carved into the stone. "Errol, look. Do ye ken what this is?" She brushed her fingers over the symbol, sweeping away dirt so they could see it more clearly.

The symbol wasn't very big, and it looked like it was carved in long after the original stone carvings were done.

Errol bent to get a better view of the symbol. "It looks like water. A wave, mayhap."

She studied it, tilting her head to the side. It did kind of look like a wave almost, which would mean water. "I believe ye are correct. Do ye ken what it could mean?"

He shook his head. "We arenae that far from the water. Could be alluding to the sea."

"The wave," she said quietly. "There has to be other symbols on the stones. Just one doesnae make sense."

Quickly, she moved to other stones, checking the back of them for any symbols that may have been carved into them. Her breath caught as she found another symbol, this time depicting a mountain peak.

Errol joined her and studied the carving, his mouth turned down in a frown. "A wave, and a mountain." He shook his head as he straightened. "It doesnae give us aught. Both are prevalent in these parts."

"There must be more."

They both began searching, looking for something else that would help them solve the puzzle.

Moira kept walking. Studying the stones. Ignoring what was written on the front since that didn't seem to matter. The symbols they'd found so far had been carved on the back of the headstones. It only made sense that if there were any additional symbols, they too, would be carved on the back.

"Moira."

She straightened at Errol's call. He had knelt behind a grave on the other side of the kirkyard.

"Did ye find something?" She asked, her feet already moving toward him.

"Aye." He dipped his head in the direction of the headstone. "Have a look for yerself."

Her eyes flashed to where he pointed, and her eyes widened. Another picture was etched into the stone.

"Is that a cave?"

Errol moved away but nodded. "'Tis what it appears to be."

Moira rubbed her hands together, thinking about all that they had found and what the clues could possibly mean.

"So," she began pacing as she spoke. "We have found a wave or water, a mountain, and a cave." She gazed at Errol, but his face was impassive as he leaned against a tree, one booted foot drawn up to rest on the thick trunk.

"Are ye aware of any caves?"

Errol gave her a droll look. "Ye cannae be serious. 'Tis Scotland, of course there are caves. Nearly everywhere ye look."

She huffed, but he had a point. Caves around Scotland were numerous. "All right. Let us ignore the caves for the moment and focus on the water symbol."

"It points to the sea."

Knitting her brows together, she waited for Errol to continue. When he didn't, she asked him of his meaning.

"How do you ken?"

He shrugged. "The carving says it all. 'Tis no' a lake. The etching shows water and waves. Ye arenae going to get waves with a loch. No' like what is depicted. That leaves the sea."

Moira rested her chin in her hand, thinking about what these symbols could mean. If they even meant aught other than a rough map of where they needed to go next.

"How long of a ride is it to the sea?" She asked.

"We could make it in a day if we pushed."

"We are missing something. There has to be another clue. These three are far too broad. As ye said, it could be anywhere in Scotland."

She paced around the graveyard once more. Walking down each row and inspecting each grave and headstone to ensure she didn't miss aught that had been left to guide them. Just as she was about to give up, she spotted a small carving, but this time it wasn't an illustration. It was words.

Loch Nunch.

"Loch Nunch," Moira said aloud. "Do ye ken where that is?"

"Aye, 'tis on our western border."

"Ye are aware of it then?"

"I just admitted to that, did I no'?"

Moira rolled her eyes, but she wouldn't be deterred. "That must be where we need to go next. Is there a cave by the sea there? With mountains in the backdrop?"

Errol remained silent and she waited impatiently for him to answer. The more time that passed, the more worried she grew that he wouldn't answer.

"There is," he said finally.

Jumping up and down excitedly, she clapped her hands.

"Well, what are we waiting for?" She asked and ignored the irritated look Errol threw her way.

CHAPTER ELEVEN

SOMEONE WAS TRACKING them. Errol had sensed it a while ago, but he was for certs of it now. He'd been listening intently and heard the tell-tale sound of twigs crunching underfoot in the distance behind them.

He'd managed to keep Moira close to his side. Not an easy task as she kept wanting to hurry ahead.

"I need ye to stay close," he ordered for the umpteenth time.

Moira only threw a droll look over her shoulder and pushed her horse forward.

He believed it was a single person. What he'd heard didn't allude to more than that. He needed to draw the man out so he could find out why he followed them. Ask him what he sought.

In a short time, they came to a small village. Located on MacLeod lands it was mainly a farming village that consisted of about twenty families. Errol could use the distraction of the bustling village to see if the man would show his face.

"We'll stop here for a brief respite."

"I think we should move forward. There's no sense in wasting time here." Moira stated as if she kenned what they should do better than he.

He raised a brow at her, letting her ken he was tired of her questioning his every move. "Ye need rest. The horses need rest. We will be on our way after a meal."

Moira looked around, her nose scrunched in the cutest way.

What was he thinking?

He was thinking that when she did that the freckles on her cheeks became more prominent. Her eyes more blue.

Errol closed his eyes and took a deep breath. She was the last thing he needed to be admiring. She was his enemy. His family's enemy.

Responsible for the death of his brother.

Why he hadn't turned them around and returned to the Macleod Keep yet was something that he still couldn't comprehend.

That was a lie. For he kenned that whilst he shouldn't, he wanted to spend as much time with Moira as he could.

They walked their horses over to a stable and handed the reins over to the stable lad that waited patiently for them.

When Errol had helped Moira dismount, he dropped his head low, whispering in her ear, "stay close."

Her blue eyes rounded, and her breath hitched. "Are they here?"

He kenned exactly who she was referring to. The bandits from earlier. But they werenae going anywhere. Errol had made sure of that.

"Nay. 'Tis but a small village and ye're safe here. However, ye still wear the Hart colors."

At that, she clutched her cloak tighter around her neck.

No one here would hurt Moira whilst she was in his presence, but that didn't stop them from throwing angry looks in her direction when they passed.

"Come. Let us sup and then we can continue on our journey to the sea."

In a small pub, they sat at a table along the far wall. Errol sat so he could see everyone that walked in the door. Whoever was following them would no doubt show themselves here as well. They ordered stew and ale, and Errol's eyes scanned the pub whilst they waited for their food.

A man entered, and Errol immediately recognized him. Their gazes clashed afore the man's slid over to Moira, a look of disgust blanketing his face.

"MacLeod," he called as he approached their table. "May I have a word?"

"Lachlan." Errol stood and acknowledged the man. He was a warrior. One of Errol's father's guards. And most likely the person that had been following them. "Ye've been trailing us for some time. Any reason?"

His gaze once again slid to Moira as he sucked on a blade of grass between his teeth.

Moira watched the exchange silently and Errol noticed she'd drawn in her cloak just a little tighter than afore. As if that would offer her any shelter from whatever attack she perceived was coming her way.

"I need a word. Alone."

Moira's eyes rounded in response, a slight shiver emanating off her body.

Errol pointed to a corner. "I will be right there. Eat yer stew. I willnae be long."

She nodded, but her eyes remained fixed on Lachlan.

Errol glanced around the small pub. No one was paying them any attention. He felt it was safe to step away from the table a few feet, and did so, Lachlan following on his heels.

Once they were out of earshot, Errol spun. "Did my father send ye here? To follow us?" His whispered words were harsh, his intention to show Lachlan that he wasn't happy with what he was doing.

"My laird doesnae ken I am here. I come of my own accord."

"For what?" Errol ground out.

"To question yer loyalty to the MacLeod. 'Tis obvious 'tis lacking if ye are working with a Hart. Does family loyalty mean naught to ye anymore?"

Errol growled. Closing the space between them. The urge to grab the man's tunic in his hands and shake him senseless was strong. He clenched his fists but remained calm.

"I would choose yer words carefully afore ye accuse me of going against my family. A family that I've shed blood for."

"And yet, here ye are with her." He nodded toward Moira, who was completely focused on their conversation. "What would yer father think if he kenned what ye are doing?"

"Are ye threatening me?"

Lachlan laughed. "Am I? God above, nay. But I fear the clan would find ye most untrustworthy if they found out ye were wandering the countryside with a Hart. What are ye doing with the wench anyway?"

Errol didn't appreciate Lachlan calling Moira a wench. He was well aware that he didn't have to answer any of Lachlan's questions. His position in Errol's father's guard did not give him any authority when it came to Errol.

"Ne'er once have I given any reason for the clan to doubt me. I willnae start now."

"Again," Lachlan waved his hand toward Moira. "I must remind ye of where ye are and with whom."

"Ye neednae remind me of aught. Return to MacLeod Keep at once," Errol demanded.

"I dinnae take orders from a traitor. Have ye forgotten what the Hart have done to us? To our clan? To our families? To *yer* family?"

Errol took a step back and pushed his hands through his short hair, dragging his nails across his scalp, allowing the pain to remind him of his duties.

"This is strictly an escort trip."

"If ye believe that, then ye are even more naive than yer sister. Ye need to take heed as to who ye let get under yer skin. Naught good can come from a Hart. She will as likely stab ye in the back when ye've turned away from her then be someone true in her actions." The man paused, his gaze falling on Moira once again, before returning to his. "She is a Hart. She cannae be trusted in aught that she does. Whate'er this mission is that ye are doing, for whate'er unkenned reason, never let yer guard down around her. If ye do, it may verra well be the last thing ye e'er do." With that, Lachlan spun on his heel and exited the pub.

Errol watched his retreat and stared at the empty doorway for a long time, thinking about what Lachlan had said. Tried to find fault in his words. But there was none. He wanted to kick himself. He'd allowed himself to get comfortable around Moira. Not completely, but moreso than afore. She'd drawn him into her impish spell, and he now realized he'd lost his way. Dragging his hands across his scalp again, he took a deep breath afore returning to the table where Moira sat watching him warily.

"Is something amiss?" She asked when he sank into the chair across from her.

"Eat. We need to be back on the road as soon as possible," he said gruffly, ignoring her question.

She must have sensed his mood shift. For once she didn't fight him and instead did as he asked. Something he hadn't seen her do yet.

He needed to keep her at arm's length. He'd promised Anna he would escort Moira around the highlands so she could find the treasure the map had alluded to. And he had his share of it that was owed to him as well. But that was all he would do. They didn't need to talk. To hold conversations, though he'd yet to find aught that they had in common to discuss anyway. Nay, this was a mission. Naught more.

Later, when he and Moira were back on their horses traveling to Loch Nunch, she'd attempted to start a conversation, filling the empty space with chatter, but he'd refused to answer. Refused to engage in anyway. Lachlan was right.

He was betraying his clan.

Moira Hart was naught but trouble. No good could come of aught betwixt them.

"What do ye think we will find in the cave?" Moira asked again, trying to fill the silence stretched thick between them.

Errol didn't answer. He just grunted and kicked his horse to move faster.

"Did I say something wrong?" Moira asked after another long silence.

Could the woman ever stop talking? It was as if she had this incessant need to fill the silence. What was wrong with enjoying the sounds of the beautiful nature that surrounded them? The babbling brook they were riding beside. The birds singing high in the trees. The rustle of the newly grown leaves, bright green on thick brown branches.

Soon, the salty brine of the sea tickled his nose. "We are almost there." He announced but said naught further.

"I can smell the salt in the air," Moira said, breathing deeply. "'Tis a beautiful smell is it no'?"

Just then, they broke through the trees and in front of them, they could see the sea, its dark blue water crashing into the rocks at the water's edge.

Moira stopped, her breath caught in her throat as she looked out at the water and its surroundings. She brought her horse forward a few steps and then turned around. "The mountain," she whispered. "The mountain, the sea," she paused. "Now we just need to locate the cave. It has to be around here, close, is it no'?"

Errol rolled his lips inward and waited for her to see the cave that was just over the rocks to their left. It was located up a steep incline and the trek getting to it would be dangerous. The rocks would be slippery, wet from the water, worn smooth from the violent waves that constantly crashed over them.

And inside?

He didn't ken what to expect. He had never explored the cave. Hadn't kenned anyone that had. The stories he had heard as a young lad was that the cave was haunted. Inhabited by a spirit who'd gone out to meet his lover on the rocks, only to be swept away afore she had appeared. Legend says he wanders the rocks now, every day, waiting for the time when his lover will appear, and they can live happily ever after.

Errol didn't believe the tale. But there were lots of others that did and for the most part it kept people away from the cave. Now that he thought about it, it was the perfect story to keep people out of a cave where something of great value had been hidden.

What better way to thwart the curious then with a ghost tale?

It had worked for him and those that he kenned. They'd all stayed far away from this cave whenever they'd been in the area.

"'Tis over there," he dipped his head to the left and waited for Moira to spot it.

When she did, her mouth formed a perfect circle. She slid off her horse and moved forward, her eyes wide.

"'Tis amazing." She spun, a huge grin splitting her face. "Have ye e'er been inside?"

"Nay," he answered and dismounted, tying his and her horses to a nearby tree.

She walked closer to the shore and paused, her hands on her slim hips. "How are we to enter it? 'Tis high."

"We will need to take caution as the rocks will be slick, but we will need to climb up to it."

"Surely there must be another way. A back entrance mayhap?" She asked, her voice hopeful.

Errol shook his head. "I'm afraid no'."

Moira clapped her hands together. "Well, then, I will just have to rely on ye and yer climbing skills, then. Too bad Rory isnae here. He would have no problem traversing those rocks."

At the mention of her brother's name, Errol's fists clenched. It was a reminder that she was a Hart and he needed to see her as naught more than that.

His enemy.

CHAPTER TWELVE

M OIRA WASN'T SURE what had happened between she and
Errol, but ever since he'd met with that man in the pub,
he'd hardly said aught to her. Just quick one or two word answers
and his eyes had turned from a warm blue to an icy gray.

She'd overheard some of the words spoken between the two
men. The man had called Errol a traitor. Had mentioned that
he'd betrayed the clan by assisting her.

She didn't think that was true at all. Aye, he was helping her,
but he'd done naught against the MacLeods. She had to work
hard to convince him to help her and when that didn't work,
Anna stepped in to assist.

But it didn't matter. She couldn't get him to talk to her. To
have any sort of lengthy conversation.

Yet, he still led them to their destination.

The area where the cave was located was breathtaking. Sitting high in the rocks, surrounded by the dark blue sea, the waves
cresting, but never reaching the opening of the cave afore they
crashed below. Even during high tide, the water line was below
the cave's entrance. She could tell because the line of the water
had left a salty line of sediment where it reached.

That had to bode well for whatever the cave hid inside. It
meant that any items inside would hopefully not be ruined by the
salty water. Behind the rock cropping, a mountain peak was just

visible, covered with trees and mounds of rocks. Just as the illustrations showed.

"Shall we?" she asked, turning to Errol who was standing off to the side, looking over the water, his jaw clenched tight. He looked as if he were fighting a war within himself.

"Ye need to stay close to my side. I'll be damned if ye fall to yer death in the sea whilst climbing to the cave."

Moira rolled her eyes. At least he had spoken two full sentences to her. Little did Errol ken she spent many years climbing trees and rocks and running across the land, much to her mother's chagrin. More than once, she'd been told her actions were very unladylike. Mayhap, but being outdoors was much more exciting than accompanying her mother in her sitting room learning how to stitch. Although, if she had learned how to stitch, she might have done a better job dealing with Errol's wound. She still felt guilty that his arm would heal with a jagged scar consisting of her uneven stitches.

They made their way down the bank to where the waves lapped the rocks and moved to the left, where rocks piled onto each other, creating an uneven slope.

"Take care, Moira. The rocks are slippery." He stepped up and turned to her, offering his hand.

Darting her tongue out to wet her lips, she looked at his outstretched hand and then met his eyes. He pulsed his hand forward, urging her to accept it.

"Come, Moira. 'Twill be easier now whilst the tide is low."

Suddenly nervous, she took a deep breath, and grasped his hand, trying to ignore the bolt of warmth that shot up her arm. With ease, he pulled her up so that she was on the same level as he. They continued on, repeating the same move over and over until soon the mouth of the cave was almost eye level.

"Just a few more steps and we will be able to climb in."

She smiled. They'd made it. Just then Moira made the mistake of looking down. Not realizing how high they had climbed, her heart jumped into her throat as her sight turned blurry. Her hand loosened in Errol's grasp, and she felt herself slipping.

"Moira!" Errol called, snapping her back to attention.

She sucked in a breath as she felt herself begin to fall. With both hands, she grappled to take a steady hold of Errol.

Strong arms wrapped around her, keeping her steady. And safe.

He was breathing heavily, his chest heaving as his eyes searched her face. "Are ye well?"

She nodded, her chin tipped up to look at him, her breath caught in her throat.

His warm body, so close to hers, emanated heat, warming her skin.

She should step away, the opening of the cave was to her right. But for some unknown reason, she found that she couldn't. She was very much enjoying the feel of his arms wrapped around her. She felt safe. Protected.

Errol didn't step away either. Nor did he loosen his hold. Instead, his eyes bored into hers before dropping his gaze to her lips.

Her breath hitched. He looked as if he wanted to kiss her. Did he? Would he?

She wanted to find out.

She tilted her head up, giving him the access to do just that if he wanted.

He bit his lower lip. His eyes tracking her tongue as once again she wet her lips. Her mouth was suddenly so dry.

And then he closed the distance, capturing her mouth in a searing kiss. He held her tighter as his tongue sought entry and she allowed it on a sigh. Opening her lips for him, she sank deeper into his hold, looping her arms around his neck.

His kiss was all-consuming, and it stole her breath.

She'd never felt any sensation such as what was being awakened in her body. Her nipples tingled and she couldn't stop herself from pressing into Errol's body, trying to create friction between them that would ease the prickling excitement.

His hands dropped to her buttocks, pulling her closer, and she could feel his hard length against her belly.

She groaned and at the sound, Errol suddenly broke the kiss, pulling away from her. He put as much distance betwixt them as he could whilst still keeping her safe.

Errol cleared his throat. He looked like he was going to say something, but instead, he snapped his mouth shut and lifted her into the opening of the cave, then climbed in behind her.

Not kenning what to say, she pressed her lips together and remained silent. She brought her fingers to her lips and could feel they were swollen from the kiss. The sensation of his soft lips still lingered.

Errol rubbed the back of his neck as he stood rigidly at the entrance. He looked like he was fighting a war within himself.

She couldn't blame him. She was sure she felt just as confused as he did. But she also wanted him to kiss her again. Was she wrong in that wanting? Mayhap. She would just keep that bit of information to herself for now.

"Shall we?" Moira asked, motioning into the mouth of the cave, trying to draw his attention away from what they'd just done.

Errol gave her a curt nod.

The position of the sun lit the interior of the cave, allowing them to see what was inside. The ceiling was high enough that Errol could stand at his full height without having to crouch over. The ground was covered with bits of dried seaweed, driftwood, and small rocks. Things that birds or creatures probably brought in over an expanse of time.

She walked carefully so she didn't twist an ankle. The air was cool, and she shivered as she trailed her hand along the wall.

"I half-expected to see a cupboard carved into the wall." She chuckled. "Like the one I found at Hartsmoor."

Errol grunted but said naught.

The cave was void of any furniture or other items that would be of use. Apparently the only inhabitants had been the animals.

"Moira, o'er here." Errol summoned her closer.

She moved deeper into the cave and stopped at his side. "What is it?"

He pointed up. "See for yerself."

Lifting her gaze, she gasped. Symbols covered the ceiling. She noticed the Hart family crest, alongside the MacLeod family crest. Intertwined arrows connected the two crests together. More clues that the Harts and MacLeods had, indeed, once been connected in some way.

"Why do ye think our families have told us for all of our lives that we are naught but enemies?"

Errol shrugged. "I dinnae ken."

She wasn't happy with that answer. "Clearly, at one time, we were no'. What do ye think happened to this couple?"

"I havenae any idea. I am seeing this for the first time just the same as ye are."

Moira fought the urge to roll her eyes. He really wasn't any different than her brothers. They would answer her questions in much the same way.

"I just dinnae understand. If, indeed, the Hart and MacLeod were joined in a marriage union…" She paused, trying to gather her thoughts and put them into words that made sense. "If they truly were, I dinnae ken why that is no' written in any of our history. I have pored o'er our historical annals, and not once have I come across aught alluding to a Hart MacLeod marriage."

"Mayhap it wasnae kenned. Or mayhap they didnae want anyone to ken. Or, and this is a big or, what if it was a forbidden union and they went against their families?"

Moira cocked her head to the side as she thought about Errol's suggestions. "I suppose that could have been the case, but how could that secret remain all these years? And why would they then go through all the trouble to create this grand chase?"

Errol sighed and leaned against the cave wall. "I dinnae have any answers for ye."

She watched him as he tried to feign interest. Her fingers

went to her mouth, remembering when Errol's lips covered hers. She would very much like to experience that feeling that flooded her body when they kissed.

Since then, he'd kept her at arm's length. Except for when he called her over to look at the paintings. Other than that, he'd kept his distance. Not initiating conversation. Leaving it up to her and only speaking when she asked him a question.

What would he do if she walked up to him right at this moment and pressed her lips to his once again? Would he wrap his arms around her? Or would he push her away? Earlier it didn't feel like he wanted to push her away. Nay, it seemed he was very much enjoying the kiss.

Just as she was.

But she wanted more. Aye, they were on a mission, but she couldn't stop thinking about the intimate moment they had shared earlier.

And she wanted to repeat it.

She took a tentative step toward him. When he didn't lift his head to look at her. She took another. Then another. Until she was standing right in front of him.

His gaze clashed with hers, his brows furrowed as he searched her face.

"Lass?" She liked it when he called her lass instead of her given name. "What is it?"

She pressed her lips together, unsure how to voice what she wanted. Would he deem her too forward if she said aloud how she wanted him to kiss her again?

Errol straightened, pulling on his neck. He looked uncomfortable with the scrutiny, but she couldn't tear her eyes away from his handsome face.

Without thinking, she lifted her hand to his cheek and stroked gently, the stubble of hair rough under her fingers.

He closed his eyes and leaned into her palm.

That meant he enjoyed her touch, didn't it? Otherwise, he would shy away from her touch, wouldn't he?

Feeling daring, she took another step and closed the distance between them so that she was nearly flush against him.

Sensing her closeness, Errol's eyes snapped open. "Lass," he warned. His voice sounded different. Strained. But his eyes blazed with amber flecks in the brown.

She stepped up on her tip toes, moving her lips closer to his. He made no move to back away. No move to stop her.

She felt emboldened.

His eyes tracked her every move and when her lips finally touched his, he lifted his hands and cupped her face, his fingers stroking along her jawline. Spinning them around, she found her back against the cool wall of the cave as he plundered her mouth as if he were starving and she were the only food around.

His tongue teased the seam of her mouth, and she parted her lips, allowing him entry. As his tongue delved inside, sweeping along her own, she brought her hands up to grasp his broad shoulders, bunching his tunic in her fingers.

A warmth grew deep in her belly, gaining strength, making her want more, but she didn't ken what that more was. She only kenned that there was something else she longed for.

Errol's hands dropped to her hips and pulled her closer, grinding his hips against her. She could feel the hard length of him, and her breath caught in her throat.

She wanted to feel his hands everywhere. Roaming over her body as if she were a map and he was the explorer ready to conquer her lands.

He broke the kiss, leaning his forehead against hers, his warm breath coming out in pants, fanning over her face.

"We cannae do this, Lass."

"I-I want to." But what was it she wanted to do? She didn't ken. She only kenned she didn't want the delicious sensations that he'd stirred within her to stop. She wanted them to keep going. To keep building. To let the inferno grow.

He groaned, rolling his hips and she sighed. "Ye fit so perfectly to my body, Lass. 'Tis a torture such as I've ne'er felt afore."

"'Tis torture for ye to stop kissing me."

He chuckled, the sound smooth as whisky rolling over her. "I want to do so much more than kiss ye, Lass."

"Then why do ye no'?"

His arms wrapped around her, and he brought her head to his chest, resting his chin upon it. "Do I really need to list all the reasons?"

"If ye are going to stop, I only feel 'tis right. I like the feel of yer lips upon mine. I want to feel them again. Is that wrong to say? To ask?"

"Nay. Aye." He sighed, the sound so loud it nearly echoed off the stone walls. "If only it were that easy. And afore ye believe aught else, I verra much enjoy the feel of yer lips. Much more than yer lips, actually. Yer body against mine feels meant to be. As if ye were created for me."

She pulled her head away from his chest to meet his eyes. "Mayhap I was."

His tongue darted out to wet his lips, and she tracked the movement. She wanted to draw it into her mouth.

"Our families, Lass."

"Families that at one time were joined. They werenae enemies. Just the opposite. We've just started to uncover the truth, but ye cannae deny it."

Errol shook his head. "I cannae. But 'tis no' that easy."

"Why no'?"

"For one, ye are Laird Hart's daughter. Do ye ken what he will do to me once he finds out that we have kissed. Or worse, lain together? Or yer brothers? But 'tis no' only them. My own father will have the same reaction."

"I dinnae understand why ye men all believe ye must continue with whate'er feud ye have conjured up in yer minds. No' a single one of ye can say why we have been fighting all these years. Why we should be fighting. Why we should remain enemies." She pushed away from Errol and grabbed his hands. "Why can we no' say enough. Why can we no' order a cease to all the fighting? End the violence betwixt our two clans. Is that too much to ask?"

Errol scraped his hands back and forth across his scalp. Then rubbed the back of his neck. "There is so much history that has happened. Ye cannae expect that to be ignored."

"It doesnae have to be ignored, but it can be addressed, can it no'?"

She took two steps back and immediately felt the absence of Errol's heat. She wanted to step right back into the warmth of his embrace, but if he was going to be stubborn as a mule, she couldn't be so close to him right now.

He would have to take the steps to change the path of their clans. And then mayhap he could convince his father. And she could go home and convince her father. And her brothers. Would that really be so hard?

"Moira." Errol's voice held a tone of longing.

She held up her hand and shook her head. "Nay. Ye have said all that I need to hear."

"Moira," Errol pled.

She held up her hands, palms out. "I dinnae need to hear aught else, Errol. I'm sorry I took liberties, I shouldnae have. 'Twillnae happen again. Please accept my apology." Moving over to the other wall, she glanced up at the paintings and noticed another arrow pointing toward the back of the cave. She looked deeper into the cave, her head tilted to the side as she studied what looked like to be the outline of a door.

Moving towards it, Errol swore behind her.

"Damn it, Moira." He pushed off the wall. "Where are ye going?"

"Continuing on our quest." She straightened her shoulders, trying to not show Errol how much his rejection had affected her. She wouldn't allow him to see the hurt she was feeling deep in her belly.

Reaching the far wall, she pushed against the stone, but it didn't budge. Her hands smoothed over the stone interior, searching for a lever or a notch or something that would open the door.

"What are ye looking for?"

Errol was standing so close behind her that she could feel his breath on the back of her neck. She could easily take a step back and be flush against his body. It took all of her might to stop herself from doing just that.

"Do ye no' see it?" She pointed to the wall.

Finally, he dragged his gaze away from hers and studied the stone, his eyes widening when he saw it. "A door."

"Aye. What do ye suppose is on the other side?"

"I dinnae ken. So far, e'erything we have found has been naught that I would have expected. So, who kens. Could be naught. Could be a treasure chest."

Moira laughed. If only that were the case. If it was a treasure chest than they could end this quest here and now and make their way back home. Errol to MacLeod Keep, and she back to Hartsmoor. For the first time, she wished for this hunt to be over, because she wasn't sure if she could sustain being so close to Errol and not being able to touch him. To act on the storm of feelings he'd awakened in her.

"There's a latch here." Errol said, his fingers wrapping around a smooth oblong stone. When he pulled, the door inched forward just a smidge. He pulled again and the door creakily swung open.

Kiss forgotten, Moira stepped forward, entering the antechamber they'd just revealed.

CHAPTER THIRTEEN

ERROL HELD BACK as Moira entered the room, rubbing his palms over his face. Jesus. How had they gotten to this position? And why, now that he'd had a taste of Moira, couldn't he now get the taste of her off his tongue? He wasn't sure he wanted to even if he could.

Moira ducked her head out. "Are ye coming?"

He grunted at the primal thoughts her simple question evoked in his mind. How he wished he were. He wanted to get lost in her soft skin. Her warm curves. Have her nails score his back. Feel her breathy moans against his neck. Hear her scream his name as she reached her climax.

Shite. He blew out a breath. He needed to change the direction of his thoughts. They would serve him no purpose.

"Well?" Moira prodded, her brows raised.

He nodded and followed her into the dark chamber, unable to see aught. "We need a torch so we can see what's inside." There was a torch near the entrance of the cave, so he exited the room and lit it, then returned to Moira.

Lifting the torch, he held it up to the walls, more faded paintings covered the ceiling and walls. Illustrations of wild beasties, birds, and fish, walking the earth, flying the sky, and swimming the lochs, told the story of the vibrant highland wildlife.

"Who did this?" Moira asked, her eyes wide as she studied the artwork.

"I dinnae ken. Someone with a lot of time to spend in caves drawing."

For a long moment Moira studied his face before smiling, a small laugh escaping her full lips. "Ye jest."

"Aye," he admitted sheepishly.

"I didnae take ye for the sort, Errol MacLeod."

"And what sort did ye think I was?"

With her head tilted to the side, Moira tapped her chin with her index finger. She looked like she was trying to figure out how to answer.

"Serious. Unyeilding," she finally answered. Then added, "bossy."

"Bossy? What are ye talking aboot? I am no' bossy."

She lifted a brow as she leveled her gaze on him.

"Och, please! Ye are one of the bossiest men I ken, and I ken a lot of them. Ye are right at the top with the rest."

He scoffed at her assessment. Not wanting to continue the conversation, he returned to studying the chamber. In multiple spots the names Hart and MacLeod were written out. Sometimes together, sometimes apart.

There appeared to be scenes depicting a story. They needed to find the beginning painting so they could make sense of what was being told.

"'Tis a story," Errol said, pointing the torch to the artwork. "If we can find the first one, we can figure out the order from there and read the story."

"I think ye are correct." Moira walked the perimeter of the cave, studying each scene before pointing to one. "I think 'tis this one."

He scanned the scene she pointed to. It showed the MacLeod and Hart clans each on their separate borders. If this truly was a story about the clans being united, it only made sense that the beginning would show them as separate entities.

"I believe ye are right. Now, let us try to decipher what 'tis trying to tell us."

For the next few hours, they went from scene to scene, slowly putting the pieces together. The clans were indeed at odds when this particular story started. That was clear by the picture depicting them each on their own lands, archers ready to shoot given the command. Swords drawn. Close to the border was a MacLeod man and a Hart woman, hands outstretched toward each other.

"'Tis the beginning of their love story," Moira said quietly, awe lacing her voice and making it soft. She pointed to the next scene. "Here, they've been wed. They're standing under a thistle-covered arch, hand in hand, two rings at their feet. That can only mean they have been united in holy matrimony, dinnae ye agree?"

Errol nodded in agreement. Moira was amazing. The rise and fall of her chest quickened with excitement at what they'd uncovered.

She moved to the next scene. "Here," she pointed. "The woman's belly is big and round. She birthed a bairn."

Visions of Moira, round with his child, filled his head and he found the image hard to shake. Just the thought of them together should be forbidden. Her belly swollen with his bairn was definitely forbidden. His eyes slid to the paintings. A MacLeod and Hart union had come to fruition afore. Why couldn't it again?

Nay. He shook his head to clear it. He and Moira would never be together. They couldn't.

"It looks like she had a wee lad." She brought her face closer to the scene to see it better, then spun to him. "If they had a son, then their lineage lived on. Do ye ken of such?"

"Nay. My da has been adamant that ye Harts are our enemies. E'en the pretty ones such as yerself."

Moira's mouth dropped open at his words.

In turn, he snapped his mouth shut, cursing to himself. Why the hell had he said that?

She pressed her lips together and then met his eyes, a smile spreading across her face. "Ye think I am pretty?" She asked coyly.

He closed his eyes and groaned. It wasn't a lie. Moira Hart was the most beautiful woman he had ever laid eyes upon. But that was something he was supposed to keep to himself, not announce it to the world.

She toed the floor of the cave with her booted foot. "Do ye?" She prodded.

Taking a deep breath, he nodded. "I do," he finally confessed.

Her smile grew wider. "Thank ye. Ye are the first person to tell me that."

He scoffed. "I cannae possibly be."

"Ye are. Well, aside from my parent's, but they dinnae count. They are supposed to say such things."

Clearing his throat, he dragged his gaze from hers and focused on the story unfolding in front of them. "What is the next scene ye can decipher?"

He felt her stare for a long moment afore she looked away. "They had the bairn and lived together in a keep. I wonder if it is MacLeod Keep. Do ye think? Mayhap an early version of it."

Approaching the scene, he studied the building. It was a square tower, similar in looks to the main building of their keep afore the various wings were added. "'Tis possible."

"I wonder if they had more children. It seems that men always want more. One isnae good enough." She added gruffness to her voice to imitate a man speaking. "Daughters serve no purpose other than as a bargaining tool. One can ne'er only have one son. What if something happens? There needs to be another to take his place."

Errol stiffened.

Moira hitched her breath, reaching out a hand to rest on his arm. "Errol, I am verra sorry. I wasnae thinking. Trying to be comical. I should ken better."

He shook her hand off. "Dinnae apologize. 'Tis fine." But her words stabbed him right in the heart. His brother, now dead and gone, was just a memory. He was the one that would have taken

Errol's place if something had happened to him that prevented him from leading the clan. Instead, without that option, even more precautions were taken with Errol. It was the only way to ensure that he would be there for the time when his father finally met his maker.

It wouldn't be in the near future. Nay, his da was strong as an ox. Big as a bear. He would remain laird for many years to come, and Errol will be there to support him.

Moira turned solemn. He believed she did truly feel bad for the words she'd said. He kenned she hadn't spoken them in spite, she was making a jest. Naught more.

"What else do ye see?" Errol asked, trying to improve Moira's mood.

Once again, a smile lifted her lips as she studied the scenes. She was enthralled with history. It was written all over her face. In the way her eyes widened when she looked at the paintings. Her excited voice when she spoke about what she'd uncovered.

It made him want to invite her to MacLeod Keep so she could spend time going through their history as well.

He scoffed. His father would never allow it.

"What is wrong?" She asked, her brows drawing down, crinkling her forehead.

He shook his head. "'Tis naught. I'm letting my thoughts take o'er."

"Do ye want to share?"

"Nay. No' now." He dipped his head toward the wall. "Have ye found aught else?"

"I only see the one child, so I dinnae believe there were any more. But this last scene." She tapped her fingertips on the picture. "The male and female are separated again. And the bairn is no longer with them." She dragged her fingers along to the last painting. "This one speaks of death. I cannae decipher if it is his, hers, or both of them. But at least one of them passed."

Moira walked the perimeter of the room. There were several small recesses carved into the stone. Carefully, she inspected each one. Making a face when she withdrew naught but spiderwebs. Wiping her hands on her skirts, she continued on.

"There is something here," she said, excitement lacing her voice as she withdrew a small bundle tied with fragile twine. "It has to be part of this. It looks similar to other items we've collected."

Errol drew closer and watched over her shoulder as Moira broke the twine away, unveiling another letter. Like the one previously, the edges of the parchment were browned with age. Delicate. It looked like it would tear or crumble easily under Moira's careful fingers. He listened as Moira read.

'Congratulations on continuing on this journey of
love's discovery.
If ye are reading this, ye will ken that though we loved with all
of our hearts, our love was not meant to be.
Instead, it was cursed. Culminating in a tragic end when we
only wanted a future together. Our blood lives on. Mayhap 'tis
ye. We fought for a future we wanted to see. We wanted to live.
But 'twas lost to us.
Mayhap ye are the one to bring us together once again.
With the hope, love, and understanding we had always
wished for.'

Her eyes met his. "It sounds like they did not have a happy ending." Her voice was sad. Quiet.

"I agree, Lass."

He opened his arms and she walked into them, nuzzling into his chest. For some reason, he felt the need to offer her comfort.

"It's as if they kenned they would fail, but they pushed on anyhow," Moira's voice cracked. "But 'twas all for naught in the end."

He stroked her hair as she worked through the emotions the story elicited. "They had hope. Sometimes, Lass, that is all that we have."

Moira pushed away from him. "Now, 'tis up to us. We are the hope that can bring their story to light."

Squeezing her tighter, he nodded. "Come on, let us sit for a bit. 'Tis been a trying day."

He pulled her to the wall and they both sank down to the ground, the coolness of the stone floor seeping through his trews.

She rested her head on his shoulder. "What do ye think happened to them?"

"I dinna ken. 'Twas many, many years ago." She swept her hand along the dirt, unveiling a carved seal. Sitting up, she swept the remainder of the dirt away. "Errol, look."

The seal was once again a blending of the Hart and MacLeod. This time, carved into the seal, was one animal—half stag, half lion—brought together to combine as one. The two prominent animals of their clans.

Moira ran her fingers along the carving, and he leaned back against the wall, resting his arm on his knee.

One thing was for certs. Their history had been built upon a lie.

Now, they just needed to uncover it.

◆—————◆

CHAPTER FOURTEEN

MOIRA STOOD UP suddenly. "We havenae searched all the recesses. There may be other items to find."

Moving to the recess nearest the one she found the letter in, she stuck her hand in and found naught but a handful of spiderwebs. Again.

She shuddered as she cleared the sticky webbing from her fingers. She hated spiders. She had her brothers to thank for that. They used to put spiders on her pillow when they were young, finding it hilarious when Moira would run screaming from her bedchamber.

It terrified Moira and she usually spent those nights wide-awake with her candle sweeping the space of her bedchamber just to see if there were any more of them wandering about in her room.

The next recess was also empty. As was the next.

But when she stuck her hand in the one after that, her fingers came into contact with something hard and wooden. She felt around the space. She had found a small chest. Her breath caught in her throat. Was this it? Was this the treasure they sought?

"Ye found something?" Errol asked from where he remained sitting on the floor watching her.

"'Tis a chest," she answered as she pulled it out into the light. It was quite heavy considering its small size.

That got Errol to his feet, and he quickly approached to assist.

The chest was small, with a hinged iron latch keeping it closed.

"Here, allow me."

"I am no' going to allow ye to take hold of the treasure," she snapped.

He rolled his brown eyes at her. "I've no plans of doing such." He reached for his dagger and brought it under the latch, turning it so it would release. Once it broke loose, he stepped back and waved his hands toward the chest. "There. I was only assisting ye with the latch. Ye are free to open it yerself and get the first look on what is contained inside."

She bit her lip, feeling guilty. They had been through a lot together on this trip. Not once had Errol overstepped his boundaries. He'd remained well-mannered, even when he had to deal with her nonsense, which was often. If her sisters were here, they would tell her that she should marry him. According to them, if she ever found a man with enough patience to deal with her antics and not take her over his knee, then he was the one she was to marry.

Moira had laughed when they'd told her, of course.

She refused to dwell on such notions.

Kneeling on the ground beside the chest, Moira lifted the lid and peered inside. Her heartbeat quickened as she took in the contents. It was full of a variety of different items.

"Look at all this." She couldn't keep the awe out of her voice. This find was amazing. It was a true treasure.

Her fingers closed around coins, and she withdrew them, stacking them in piles beside her. A jeweled necklace bedecked with a large ruby. Moira was tempted to put it around her neck, but thought twice about it, her mind going to the curse mentioned in the missive they found earlier. Could a necklace be cursed?

She assumed it could be and set it to the side. She didn't want to take any chances. There was a matching bracelet and ear baubles with smaller rubies that would dangle from her lobes—if her ears were pierced—which they weren't. A stag figurine carved out of white stone. A lion carving, as well.

A figurine matching the seal they found in the floor was next. Half stag, half lion. It was such an odd combination, but it made perfect sense. It was the blending of their two clans.

Everywhere they looked, the union was alluded to. So, what was it that caused them to part?

At the bottom of the chest there were more coins. She removed them and stacked them near the other ones. When she got to the last few coins, she paused. At the bottom of the chest, laying flat on the red velvet interior was what appeared to be another letter.

"Errol, look."

He leaned over her and peered into the chest. "Is that another letter?"

"It looks to be. Does it no'?"

"Aye."

Moira picked it up and clasped it to her chest. "What do ye think it says?"

He shrugged. "Mayhap 'twill tell the rest of the story."

Her heart felt excited and heavy at the same time. Excited that she found another letter, but sad to ken that she might finally learn the tragedy that had been told in the scenes from earlier. She wasn't sure she was ready to hear it.

It was funny. She felt a connection to this couple. She didn't ken them. She didn't even ken their names, other than their surnames. But, yet she found herself drawn to them. To their story. To their love. To their lives which were cut short way too early. Or at least one of their lives had.

"Are ye going to read it?" Errol asked. Was that impatience she heard in his tone? Mayhap he was just as curious in finding out the rest of the story as she was.

"Aye." There was no twine wrapped around this letter. It was neatly folded into a rectangle and appeared to be much sturdier than the other's she had found. That was more than likely due to it being stored away at the bottom of the chest. The enclosed space and lack of air helped to preserve the integrity of the parchment. It was also much larger than the other letters and consisted of several pages.

She began reading aloud. Beside her, Errol listened intently. The couple had met by chance at a small burn that ran between their two lands. Immediately attracted to each other, they secretly rendezvoused often. Meeting at the burn. At the loch, which was on Hart land, where they would swim together, enjoying the sun and the coolness of the water. Stealing kisses. Touches. Caresses.

Moira sighed. It all sounded so very romantic.

Soon, the woman, whose name was Fiona, was with child. Thomas, the man, insisted they wed. He would not have his bairn be born out of wedlock.

They approached their families and were shunned by both. But when their heads had cleared and open minds prevailed, they thought about what a bairn between a Hart and a MacLeod would mean.

Peace.

Unity.

The couple were given a small parcel of land between the two clans. Their land would act as a bridge of peace bringing the two clans together. By the time the bairn was born, communications amongst the clans had opened up. Whilst they had never been fierce enemies afore, they had never really teamed up together either. This union closed that gap. The two clans joined.

As a united front, they became a formidable force to be reckoned with amongst the other clans in the area.

Moira paused for breath, soaking in the information they'd learned so far.

"This letter is giving us the full history," Errol said, shaking his head. "Back then we werenae enemies. We were one. Fighting side by side. I dinnae believe it."

"Ye must." She held up the letter, shaking it in the air. "'Tis all written here. It has been here all along, just waiting for it to be found." She took a deep breath. "I am almost scared to read on. Right now, they are happy, bringing peace across the land. I ken when I read on, that will all be shattered. And I dinnae wish to see that."

Errol drew Moira close to his side and gently kissed the top of her head. She closed her eyes, savoring his touch. His scent. When had she crossed the line in seeing Errol as more than just Anna's older brother? Seeing him as more than a means to an end.

She wasn't sure, but she kenned that now that she had gotten a taste of what it felt like to be in Errol's arms, she never wanted to be in the position where he wasn't nearby ever again.

"Ye ken that things dinnae end well for them. We've already learned that. We just dinnae ken the why and how of it. I am sure that by the time ye finish reading we will have those answers."

"But I am no' sure I want those answers."

He smiled and tipped her chin up to him. His eyes bore into hers for a long moment before they dropped to her lips. She darted her tongue out, wetting them. She suddenly felt parched, but not for ale. Would he kiss her?

He looked like he wanted to.

Did she want him to?

Aye. She did. Very much so.

"Kiss me, Errol," she whispered.

"I shouldnae, Lass," he said quietly. "But I find the more time I spend in yer presence, the less control I have to deny ye."

With that, he dipped his head and captured her lips in a searing kiss that she felt all the way to the tips of her toes. He groaned when she opened her mouth, allowing his tongue entry. He ran it along the seam of her lips afore sweeping it into her mouth and their tongues twisted against each other in a seductive dance that Moira wanted more of.

When they parted, they were both gasping for air, their chests rising and falling with each ragged breath.

"As much as I am enjoying the taste of yer lips, Lass, we need to stop." He pointed to the parchment she still clasped in her hands. "We need to finish their story."

"Mayhap I want to continue *our* story."

He chuckled, the sound foreign to her ears. But she found she enjoyed it and wanted to hear it again.

"As do I," he admitted and she wanted to clap in victory, but she remained still, watching the struggle play across his face. She kenned he was waging a war within himself.

She had too, but gave in long ago, understanding that she would never be able to let this man go.

"If we continue whate'er is building betwixt us, 'twill no' be done in a cave."

"When we continue," she corrected him.

He kissed her on the nose. "Aye. When."

Happy with his answer, she turned and leaned her back against his chest once again and focused her attention back on the letter, dreading what she kenned was not going to be the happy ending she wanted for the couple. No matter how much she wished for it, their tragedy had already happened. It couldn't be changed now.

"Continue," Errol urged.

Moira found the spot she'd left off and began reading again. The letter talked about the son they'd borne. And a daughter.

Her and Errol's gazes clashed, his mouth turned down in a frown. "A daughter? We didnae see any mention of a wee lassie being born, did we?"

Moira shook her head. "There wasnae any word about another bairn, laddie or lassie."

'Our dear daughter, Agnes, was a lovely lass.
Full of sunshine, she brightened the room wherever she went.
But we ne'er could have fathomed the untimely death she
would meet.'

"I dinnae like where this is going," Moira confessed, but continued reading.

' 'Twas a warm summer day and Agnes was playing in the
woods near our home.
Her brother, Angus, was busy helping their father in the fields.
They returned, but Agnes didn't. We set out to find her.
It took hours. But we finally found her broken body.
Dead at the bottom of the cliffs near the sea.'

Moira gasped. "Nay! Their daughter died," she cried, overcome with sadness. "How tragic and devastating. I really dinnae like this now."

"Nor do I, but we must continue on. 'Tis the only way we will learn the whole history of our clans. The only way we will be able to mend the pain of the past. Our past."

'What we thought was an accident, we soon learned the
dire truth.
One that would put our clans at war.
A clansman from one of the border clans had taken our
precious lass.
Infatuated with her.'

With sorrow and anger running through her blood, Moira finished reading the heartbreaking story of Agnes and her death at the hands of someone who stole her virtue and her life, discarding her like rubbish on the rocks.

As if that weren't enough, the clan responsible created a false narrative surrounding the actual happenings. They killed Thomas, leaving Fiona to deal with the ramifications. They swore an oath that Fiona was the cause for the deaths of her family members. The MacLeod's took possession of Angus and sent her back to the Harts, and shunned her and her clan. But worse, her clan also turned their backs on her, banishing her from the land she and Thomas had been gifted. The same land they'd built a life upon. A happy life—until it wasn't.

She tried to speak the truth, but no one would listen. They hated her for what she represented. Hated her for the shame she brought on the clan. Hated her for the way she broke the peace. They wouldn't believe that she wasn't the one responsible. It mattered naught how many times she tried to explain.

She mourned alone, roaming the land.

Kenning the only way the truth would ever come to light, she painted their story on the cave, hid the clues, mementos, and treasures throughout the highlands. Kenning one day, someone would find what she'd done, and the truth would be brought to light.

There was still one, final treasure to be found.

'Where the cliffs meet the sea. Where sand meets salt.
Trees shade the sun. Find the hollow.
Learn the truth.'

Moira swept at the tears that welled in her eyes. "How tragic," she repeated.

Errol pinched the bridge of his nose. "We've still got one more location to discover, but from what we've learned so far, our whole history of being enemies has been based on naught but lies." He pushed off the floor and paced the interior of the cave. "We need to go."

HE PACED THE banks of the shore far below the cave where Errol and Moira had disappeared into hours ago. Irritation had him clenching his fists.

He couldn't see what they were doing or what they had found, if aught.

He couldn't hear their conversation.

The only thing he could do was wait for them to exit and

continue on to wherever they needed to go next. His stupid leg wouldn't allow him to climb the rocks leading up to the cave and there was no other way to get to it. He was stuck here.

Waiting.

Waiting.

Waiting.

He growled, pulling his hair until pain seared his scalp.

Stupid.

Stupid.

Stupid.

He slapped his face. Again and again as his father's words echoed in his head.

"Ye useless dolt. Ye are naught but a curse. A liability. A disappointment." That last statement stung the most.

He squeezed his eyes shut and covered his ears as he rocked back and forth, trying to drown out the voice of the man who had not once ever offered him comfort.

Still, he would come out victorious in this mission. He just needed to be patient.

Making his way back to the trees, he sank onto the ground, leaning his back against one of the thick trunks. He would sleep here tonight, waiting for Errol and Moira to emerge. When they did, this vantage point would allow him to see them as soon as they did.

Chapter Fifteen

T HEY LEFT THE cave just afore dawn. The mist rolling off the water covered the ground below them as Errol and Moira carefully maneuvered their way back down to the rocks and back to their waiting horses.

Errol didn't ken what to do with all of the information they had just uncovered.

The lies.

Everything was built on a lie.

What the hell was he supposed to do with that revelation?

Had his clan really dismissed Fiona's explanation of the events that had led to her to seek solace with the MacLeods?

Aye.

They clearly had. And that information had been used to fuel the feud between them for years and years.

Once they had safely descended and their feet were on solid ground, Errol pulled the small chest from his tunic. He had tied off the cloth to act as a sling to support the chest whilst they climbed down.

He set it on the ground and fixed his tunic, so it covered him once again.

Errol hadn't missed the way Moira's eyes had lingered on his bared stomach.

She hadn't said aught. She didn't have to. Her eyes said everything.

He kenned where they needed to go next. There was only one spot on MacLeod lands that had cliffs leading to the sea with a nearby hollow.

Exhaustion seeped into his bones. It felt like he hadn't slept for days and if he was tired, Moira surely had to be.

They would pass a village on the way to the cliffs. They could stop there for food and rest.

She needed to sleep. He refused to be blamed for not providing Moira adequate lodging and sustenance whilst she was in his care.

The horses neighed as they drew close. Errol gave them a quick look over to ensure they hadn't come to any harm in the hours they'd been away. He smoothed his hand over his horse's muzzle, then ran his hand down his mane and over his muscular flank.

He tucked the chest in his bag draped over the horse's back then turned to help Moira mount her mare.

She'd been silent ever since they'd exited the cave and he kenned she was thinking about the letter. Thinking about Fiona. About Agnes.

He couldn't blame her. He was, too.

"Do ye ken where we need to go?" Her voice was quiet. Small.

The opposite of what he'd come to expect from her when she spoke. She was always strong and sure in her words. Suddenly, she seemed, what was the word he was searching for?

Vulnerable. That was it.

She looked vulnerable.

He nodded. "I do. But ye need rest. We'll stop in the village we will pass on the way by."

"I dinnae need to—"

He cut her off by holding up his hand. "Ye do and ye will. It's been a trying night. We havenae slept for some time, nor have we eaten."

As if on cue, her stomach rumbled loud in the clearing in which they sat atop their horses.

He lifted a brow in question at her. "It seems to me yer stomach is betraying ye. I find I am also quite hungry. We'll sup. Rest and be fresh to finish this quest. How does that sound?"

She twisted her mouth, not wanting to admit that he was right, but she finally nodded.

"Mayhap we can e'en order baths."

Her eyes lit up at that and she sat a little straighter on her horse. "That would be nice."

BY THE TIME they arrived in the village and made their way to the inn and secured a room, Moira's eyes had grown heavy with sleep.

He'd watched her closely whilst they rode, ready to step in if he thought she would fall or not be able to continue on. But she persevered and pushed through.

She was strong. He wondered if she realized that about herself.

Now that they'd arrived, she breathed a sigh of relief as they were led to their room, their single room, and fell onto the bed, sinking into the soft pile of throws.

Errol had indeed convinced the innkeeper to prepare baths for them. Of course, he insisted Moira bathe first. When she was done, he'd take his turn.

For a moment when securing the room, he had hesitated on renting only one room. It had been a trying couple of days. The information they'd uncovered had heavy emotional ramifications. He didn't want her to stay alone.

If she needed comfort, he wanted to be the one to offer it to her, even though he kenned he shouldn't be.

He sighed, thinking about the revelations they'd learned. Aye, everything he'd kenned growing up was built on a lie. He could explain that to his father. Even show him proof, however, doing that wouldn't be enough to erase decades of hate toward the Harts.

They'd killed his brother.

He couldn't forgive them for that.

Ever.

A knock on the door brought his attention back to the room and he answered, allowing the maids carrying buckets of water to enter and fill the tub. They kept returning until the basin was three-quarters of the way full and steam filled the room. They even provided a bar of soap scented with dried lavender afore they left.

Once he and Moira were alone, he rubbed his hands together. "I will leave ye to bathe in peace. Do ye need aught from me afore I go?"

Her eyes clashed with his. "Where will ye go?"

"The tavern next door. I could use a whisky. Mayhap e'en two." He smiled. "But if ye need something afore I go, I will get it for ye."

She pushed off the bed and crossed her arms, her palms rubbing her upper arms. "Ye brought my bag in, so I have all that I need." Moving to the tub, she dipped her fingertips in. "The water is perfect." She picked up the soap and breathed in its scent, closing her eyes on a sigh. "It smells divine."

Errol nodded. "Right. Well, I shall leave ye to it. Latch the door behind me, Lass. Dinnae open it for anyone but me."

She eyed him. "Whoe'er do ye think I would allow into our room?"

He shrugged. "I dinnae ken." And he didn't. She didn't ken anyone here, but still felt the need for the warning. He didn't want aught to happen to her. He didn't think he would ever be able to forgive himself if harm came to her on his watch. But it wasn't just that. Moira meant something to him. She'd whittled away at his heart on this journey. Chipping away his walls piece by piece until it was just a sliver left, and then, she'd chipped that away as well. "I dinnae believe ye would let anyone else in, but one can ne'er be too cautious. We are still on MacLeod lands, and ye are still a Hart. None of these people ken aught about what we've found. As far as they are concerned, ye are still the enemy."

She grimaced at that reminder. Then shooed him towards the door. When he turned in the hall to face her, she said, "I promise I willnae open the door for anyone but ye."

Satisfied, he pulled the door closed and waited for the telltale sound of the latch engaging. Once it had, he made his way down the hall and out the door to the nearby tavern.

The smoke-filled room smelled of soot, stale whisky, and spilled ale. That should bother him more than it did. But he was parched. The whisky could taste like dirty water, and he would probably still drink it.

He found a seat and sat down. Within moments, a serving wench with long red hair plaited down her back, big green eyes, and an even bigger bosom greeted him with a sway of her wide hips. When she smiled, her grin revealed a missing tooth.

Errol didn't spend much time in this part of MacLeod lands and therefore didn't recognize any familiar faces. The serving wench was no exception.

"What can I get ye?" She drawled, licking her lips as her eyes slid down his body and then back up again. She cocked her hip to the side and jutted out her chest. He was sure that her actions probably worked on some men that wandered in here, but they had no effect on him whatsoever.

But kenning that Moira was up in their room, naked, her perfect, pale skin slick with water? That was a sight he would pay coin to see.

"Whisky," he answered.

The wench stayed by his table, instead of going and fetching his order. When he said naught further, she asked, "Aught else?" She bent over and placed her palms on the table, which gave him an uninhibited view of her hefty bosom thanks to the low neckline of her gown. She formed her lips into a pout.

"Nay. Just the whisky."

"Are ye for certs? Ye're a braw man. I bet ye could use—"

He didn't let her finish whatever she was going to say. "I said nay. Just the whisky. Now."

Her green eyes widened at his terse voice, and she straightened. "I will be back shortly."

He ignored her hurt expression at his rejection. He had the most beautiful woman he'd ever laid eyes upon in his room at the inn. The thought of a toss with a serving wench, this one in particular, was not in any way appealing.

He wondered if Moira's breasts were bobbing in the water of the tub. He groaned, running his palms over his face.

Those were thoughts he didn't need to be thinking. He needed to remain strong. Remember his duty to his clan and his father.

Moira, pretty as she was. Attractive as she was.

She was still a Hart. And there was no getting around that.

Chapter Sixteen

THERE WAS NAUGHT more luxurious that a hot, scented bath after days of traveling. Moira felt refreshed as she ran a brush through her hair and then plaited it into a thick braid that she then looped into a bun and fastened it with pins.

Errol had bathed in another room and once he had finished, he returned to their room, and they went to supper. Clean and with a full belly, she was content.

But now she faced a dilemma, staring at the one bed that was the main focus of the room. Of course, they had been in the situation afore, but she had Seema with her then, and Errol slept on the floor. They've also been alone since Seema returned to MacLeod Keep. They had spent the night together at the bothy as well. But Errol had been injured and then they fought, and he had slept in the chair. She still felt guilty about that.

She didn't understand her hesitation with their one bed situation now. The majority of this journey has just been the two of them.

So, it was silly that she was feeling the way she was. Nervous. As if this were the first time she was seeing Errol.

They'd kissed. Multiple times. Moira brought her fingertips up to her lips. She could still feel the warmth of Errol's mouth.

She wanted to experience that feeling again.

Mayhap that was the reason she felt on edge. Conflicted. Like

Errol was a piece of forbidden fruit that she wasn't allowed. He had told her more than once the reasons why they couldn't be together.

And then there was the death of his brother. His family clearly blamed her clan for the attack, even though Moira could say with certainty that it wasn't them. But years of believing something didn't just disappear overnight. If that was what he truly believed, then it was his right to harbor such angry feelings toward her.

Yet, Errol had been naught but kind and gentlemanlike. Even at the start of their journey when he was grumpy because he didn't want to assist, he still made sure she was safe and taken care of. He'd kept to himself, erecting walls to keep her out, but slowly, he'd been letting them down.

Yestereve, in the cave, those walls had crumbled. She got a glimpse of his soft, caring side.

And she liked it. A lot. He was endearing and thoughtful. And chivalrous. He had saved her from falling onto the rocks whilst they climbed. If she had slipped it surely would have meant her death.

But as they supped, she saw those walls building up again. She didn't understand why. He'd shut down almost all of their conversations, telling her to finish her meal so they could return to the inn and rest afore continuing on.

The door opened and Errol walked in, his arms stacked with folded throws.

"What are ye doing?" she asked, sitting up straighter on the bed.

He gave her a droll look. "Making the floor a wee more comfortable to sleep on."

"Errol." She rolled her eyes. "Dinnae be ridiculous. Ye can sleep in the bed."

"Absolutely no'."

By the stubborn set of his jaw, she could tell that there was no way to sway Errol's mind. Instead of trying to fight with him about it or convince him otherwise, she went to him and picked up a throw.

Unfolding it, she shook it out to lay it flat on the floor. Errol helped by snatching the opposite corners, making it easier to spread. Then they did the same for the next one. Grabbing a pillow off the bed, Moira added it to the makeshift pile.

"It doesnae look verra comfortable."

"'Twill be fine. I have slept on worst."

"The bed is plenty big. We wouldnae e'en touch each other if ye slept there."

"I willnae. The bed is yers." He ran his hands along his scalp. "'Tis no' up for discussion."

When she just stood there watching him, he sighed.

"Go to bed, Moira." His voice was gruff.

She opened her mouth to say something, but he stopped her with a lift of his large hand.

"Enough. Go to bed," he ordered.

Irritated, she spun and sat down on the bed. "If you want me to get ready for bed, ye need to afford me my privacy to do so." Her voice was snippy and clipped, but she didn't care.

"Gladly. I shall be outside."

Moira watched Errol as he shut the door behind him with a slam.

She hadn't meant for him to leave the room completely. He could have just turned his back. She blew out an exasperated breath and fell back on the bed, covering her eyes with her arm. She would never understand men. After this trip, she didn't plan to even try any more. It was a useless feat truth be told.

A knock sounded and she heard Errol through the door ask if she was ready.

"I havenae e'en started," she answered back.

"Then ye should make haste."

"Mayhap ye shouldnae tell me what to do," she countered.

"Or mayhap, if ye dinnae finish up in three minutes, I will just walk into the room anyhow."

She sucked in her breath. He wouldn't dare. Would he?

"Test me," he called from the other side of the door as if he had read her mind.

Quickly she stripped out of her gown and into her shift, then hastily slipped under the blankets, drawing them up to her chin so that when Errol opened the door he would only see her head.

Just as he'd warned, he walked in without a care for whether or not she was dressed.

She pressed her lips together as she watched him move about the room. First, he stoked the fire in the fireplace and added another thick log, so they would be set for the night. Then he sat in the chair and watched the dancing flames for a few minutes afore he removed his boots.

He stood and pushed his trews down, his tunic fell mid-thigh, covering his buttocks, but she could see the muscles of his shapely legs. Strong legs that had been honed into hard muscle from hours upon hours of training.

Holding her breath, Moira waited for Errol to remove his tunic, but to her disappointment, he kept it on, extinguished the candle and climbed between the throws on the floor.

For a long time, she lay there quietly, until she couldn't stand it anymore.

"Errol?"

He sighed. "Aye?"

She smiled, she kenned he hadn't fallen asleep, but then grew serious when she thought about what she was going to ask him, unsure if she really wanted to hear the answer.

"Is something amiss? Did I do aught wrong?"

"Nay."

One word. That was all he said. Of course, she wasn't happy with that answer and pushed on. "I dinnae believe ye. Ye've hardly said aught to me today. After the day we spent yesterday, it doesnae make sense. Surely I have done something to upset ye."

"Moira, cease and let it go."

"I willnae. I realize we havenae spent a lot of time together, but we have spent enough that ye should ken me better than that. What has changed?"

She heard him blow out a long breath.

"Naught has changed. I only realized that what we were doing was foolish and something that cannae continue."

"Why no'? Ye cannae tell me that ye didnae enjoy our kisses, Errol MacLeod."

"That is the reason why. I shouldnae have been enjoying them as much as I did. Need I remind ye that ye are a Hart? In no circumstance would what we have done be acceptable. 'Tis easier if we cease now, afore either of us get hurt."

But it was too late for that. She was already hurting. Missing his touch. His kiss. His strong arms wrapping her in a warm embrace.

"On the morrow we will ride to our destination and then we are done with this wild chase. Ye will return home to Hartsmoor, and I will return to MacLeod Keep and life will go on as it was afore."

"Can ye really just forget about what has happened betwixt us that easily?"

"Naught happened, Moira. Naught that mattered anyway."

She gasped at his bluntness. He was lying. He had to be. She'd felt the caring in his touch. Seen the softness in his eyes. Those were real. And they meant something. He may not want to admit it, but it was true.

Even truer was the stabbing pain she felt at his admission. Like she had just been punched in the stomach.

Swiping at the tear that slipped from her eye, she clenched her fists. She refused to let him see how he affected her.

Nay, she didn't need him to continue on. He had told her of the location whilst they supped earlier. She only needed to go Northeast, and it would take her to the final destination. She would find the final clue without him.

Being the bigger person, she would uphold her end of their

deal and ensure that he gets the percentage of the treasure they had agreed upon, but other than that? There would be naught.

As she waited for Errol to fall asleep, a plan formed in her mind. Once she was certain he was asleep and would not wake, she would slip out of bed, quietly dress, then grab her bag and leave the room, hoping that the door would not creak and awaken him.

It seemed to take hours, but finally Errol's breathing evened out, and every so often, he let out a soft snore, which she found endearing. But she couldn't think about that. He wanted them to keep apart? Well, she would help him along with that.

Once dressed, she gathered her bag and tip-toed to the door, taking care to make as little noise as possible. Just as she was about to disengage the latch, she remembered that she didn't have any coin. Errol had been paying for everything so far. Traveling alone, she would more than likely come across something that she would have to pay for.

Leaving her bag near the door, she crept over to Errol's bag and found the coin pouch he had tucked inside. She could take the whole thing with her and leave him with naught. Being the son of the laird, he would have no problem getting around, but she wasn't spiteful.

Instead, she took a small handful and tucked the coins into her pocket, trying to minimize the jingling noise they made as they rubbed together.

Carefully opening the door, she said a silent prayer when it made no sound, and then she slipped outside into the dark, empty hall.

Downstairs, she breathed a sigh of relief when even the inn-keeper was nowhere to be found. Mayhap he had retired for the night as well.

Outside, she located her horse in the stable, and handed the sleepy-eyed stable boy a coin for watching and caring for the mare.

He looked confused as he tried to rub the sleep out of his

eyes, but she told him that all was well and to go back to sleep. Nodding, he had curled back up on a bale of hay and fell back asleep.

Usually, she had Errol to help her mount, but of course, she was on her own this time. She found a stool and moved it over beside her horse and stepped upon it, then, using the reins, pulled herself the rest of the way up, careful not to hurt her mare.

Outside of the stable, she urged her horse left and once she was certain no one followed, she kicked the mare into a trot and headed in what she hoped was Northeast. According to what Errol had said, it should only take but a few hours to arrive at the hollow.

Moira tried not to think about how her father would react if he kenned she were traveling MacLeod lands by herself.

She shuddered. She hadn't thought about that piece until now. Mayhap she should take off her cloak since it was in the Hart colors. That way she didn't catch anyone's ire if they happened upon her.

Thinking that was best, she untied the bow at her neck and slipped the cloak off her shoulders. Rolling it into a ball, she stuffed the cloak under her leg. She would put it in her travel bag when she stopped next, which would be when she got to the hollow.

Errol would be furious when he woke up to find himself alone in the room. Not because he cared about her, but because he wasn't keeping up with the responsibility of being her guardian.

Well, she would show him. She didn't need a guardian and she could travel just fine alone.

At least that was what she kept repeating to herself.

He was awakened by the movement in the stable. He had been

sleeping outside, near the blacksmith's shed. It gave him a view of the stable and the horses inside. Though he was surprised to see the Hart bitch fetching her mare.

He was even more surprised to see that she was alone.

What was she up to?

He had waited to see if the MacLeod followed her, but once she'd mounted her horse and left the stables with no sign of him, it was clear she was stealing away in the night and leaving him behind.

That was fine with him. She would be much easier to track. She didn't take care to cover her tracks like the MacLeod.

He mounted his horse, and set off to follow Moira Hart, keeping a wide enough distance that she wouldn't hear his horse trailing behind her.

Where was she going without her escort?

Her *protection*.

She was moving Northeast. But to where? Eventually, she would end up at the sea, unless she veered off in another direction.

Was she after another clue? He still had not learned what they had found in the hidden cave. But he had seen the small chest the MacLeod had carried with him down the rocks. What contents it held he had no idea. It could be empty for all he kenned, but he doubted that. Why would he burden himself with an empty chest whilst he climbed down a precarious rock wall?

He wouldn't do that.

Nay. There had to be something valuable inside.

Ahead of him, Moira's mare paused, and he signaled for his horse to do the same thing, stroking its neck to keep him at ease so he remained silent.

Whatever caused her to stop had passed and she once again moved forward.

Into the trees he followed her, the branches reaching out and scratching at his face. He swiped them out of the way. Swearing when one poked him in the eye, pain stabbing into his socket.

Thankfully, she hadn't heard him, and she continued on as if she didn't have aught to be worried about.

He hated the woods. They reminded him of when he and his brother would play when they were young. His brother nimbly jumping over fallen trees and logs, running swiftly away as they would chase each other. He could never catch his brother.

But his brother always caught him. Not right away. His brother had always given him a lead start and didn't put in a lot of effort. There was no use since the chase would always end the same way.

His brother was a good man. And for the briefest of moments, he felt a pang of sadness. Of guilt.

The way his father always doted on his brother was sickening. Just once, he wanted to be the subject of his father's devotion.

Only once.

But it never came to fruition.

His father was a mean, selfish bastard.

He had learned of their family's secret through his brother.

His brother that should have taken over the family land on their father's death.

He sneered.

He took care of that.

Remembering when his father had fallen onto a jagged branch when riding. His brother had been dead for a few weeks by that time. His father was still grieving the loss of his beloved son.

It made him sick.

But when his father fell, he kenned he had his chance. He found a nearby rock, hefty enough to do the job he sought.

His father had called out to him, asking for help.

He laughed. "Now I am of use to ye, ye old fool?"

Confusion furrowed his father's brow, seeing the rock in his hand.

He bent near his father, leaning down to whisper in his ear.

"Ye thought I was useless. But, yet I managed to strike down yer son, did I no'?"

His father's eyes rounded, understanding dawning on his face.

"Aye. 'Twas me. I am no' so useless now, am I?"

"Son," his father said.

"Dinnae call me that," he spat, spittle falling from his lips and onto his father's cheek. "Ye dinnae get the privilege of calling me that after all these years." He bent once again, his mouth near his father's ear. "Just ken that he suffered, I made sure of it."

He stood and saw the pain in his father's eyes. The anger. Reveling in the knowledge that his father could do naught about it, he brought the rock down onto his father's skull with all his might. He struck again and again, until he couldn't see his father's face anymore. Just tissue and bone and blood.

Dropping the rock, he left his father where he had fallen. The scavengers would make use of his remains.

He didn't deserve a burial.

Bringing his focus back to the here and now, he watched Moira's figure in the far distance, wondering where she was going for the umpteenth time. Would this be the final clue? If it were, he would be able to dispose of her, just like he had his father and his brother. And then he would destroy the clues and keep the family secret.

It mattered naught what happened to him. There was no one left in his family. With no wives and no children born to his brother, their lineage died with him.

But he had the last laugh. The final victory.

It was him.

He was the one to keep the family secret safe.

CHAPTER SEVENTEEN

ERROL WOKE AFORE the sun had risen, not able to sleep any longer. He stretched his arms above his head and cracked his back. The two blankets below him were more comfortable than sleeping on the bare floor, but they offered little comfort still. His bones were weary.

He didn't look forward to the ride he and Moira would set on later. His body would scream in protest. But if all went well, they would find what they were looking for and then return home where he would spend the day in a nice hot bath and then mayhap losing himself in a wench who would first massage the bunches out of his tired muscles.

He scoffed. He didn't want another woman touching him.

Now Moira? He would love to lose himself in her. To have her rub away his aches and pains. Her small hands roving over his body. The thought was divine.

But he couldn't. No matter how much he wished for it to be so, it couldn't happen. That's why he'd done what he had the night afore. If he made her hate him, it would be much easier to let her go. She wouldn't want to stay near him.

And that's what he needed. He needed her to not want to be near him.

To not like him.

To see him as the enemy.

To hate him.

But it hurt kenning that he had upset her.

He sat up and then stood. He was moving toward the table to grab a cup of ale when he stole a glance toward the bed. Moira was beautiful when she slept, and against his better judgement, he wanted to see her slumber again. It was usually when she looked most peaceful.

But the bed was empty where Moira was supposed to be. She wasn't there.

"What the hell?" He said to the empty room, looking around. His gaze fell to his travel bag, sitting alone. He had set Moira's bag beside his when they'd retired for the night.

"Shite!"

What had she done?

"I ken exactly what she has done," he grumbled into the empty room as he pulled his trews on. He had pushed her away last eve. That was his plan. In his mind, doing so would stop her from pursuing aught betwixt them. In no way did he think she would leave to continue on her own. He should have kenned better. The lass was stubborn as a mule.

He shook his head as he stuffed his feet into his boots. Grabbing his bag, he rushed out the door and down the stairs.

The innkeeper was nowhere to be found. Errol assumed he wouldn't be able to help him anyway, so he left the inn and made his way to the stables, kenning when he got there that Moira, and her mare would be absent.

The stable boy jumped up from the hay bale he had been sleeping on at Errol's sharp voice.

"Did Lady Hart fetch her horse?"

"Aye, my laird," he answered quickly.

"How long ago?"

The lad shrugged. "'Tis been under two hours, I would say. No' more than that."

"Which way did she leave?"

He shook his head, his long, brown hair swaying back and

forth. "I didnae see." He dropped his eyes, his shoulders slumping. "I am sorry, my laird. I should have stopped her."

Errol pinched the bridge of his nose. He hadn't meant to upset the lad. It seemed like that was all he had been doing lately—upsetting people.

"There is naught for ye to apologize for. Here." Errol reached into his coin purse and withdrew a coin and gave it to the wide-eyed boy. "Thank ye for taking care of our horses."

Saddling Dubh Bàn quickly, Errol left within minutes. The lad may have not seen where Moira was headed, but he kenned.

Northeast.

Errol had no doubt if he headed Northeast, he would catch up to Moira. He could ride faster than she and even if she had a two-hour lead on him, he could get to her in half the time. He was sure of it. His horse was fast, and he would push him to his limits.

There was a half-moon hanging low in the sky, lighting enough of the ground in silvery brightness to see the ground in front of him.

His horse was sure-footed as they thundered out of the village and into the woods that would lead them to the sea and their last destination.

The whole time he rode, he fashed that he would come across Moira's crumpled body after being thrown off her horse. The further he rode on, the more relieved he was that he didn't see that.

But lord above, what was she thinking riding alone? Not just alone, but at night as well? Traveling alone as a lady during the day was dangerous enough. Adding the anonymity of darkness and the danger multiplied ten-fold. Not only that, she was a Hart riding alone through MacLeod lands. Errol didn't want to think about what would happen to her if she came upon some MacLeod men in the woods.

He made a silent plea that she was safe and hadn't met any harm. He wouldn't be able to forgive himself if something happened to her. It didn't matter that she was out of his care at the time.

At no point on this journey was she supposed to be anywhere but in his care. Under his guardianship. If he couldn't manage that, her brothers and father would surely see him hang.

Noticing the trampled pine needles and crushed leaves on the ground, he was sure he'd found Moira's trail. He frowned. It looked to him like there were two travelers. Had she met up with someone? Or mayhap she hired someone to escort her to the next destination. Nay. He didn't believe that to be the case. Firstly, she didn't trust easily, which was a good thing. But, secondly, she didn't have any coin to pay anyone to escort her.

He supposed she could have promised them part of the treasure she would uncover, but after the attack they suffered previously, all in the name of those who were after the treasure, he didn't think she would speak so freely of what her intentions were.

That left the option that someone was following her.

His heart picked up speed and he gripped the reins tighter. Moira could be in grave danger. He had to get to her fast. Driving his heels into Dubh Bàn's side, he urged the horse to push harder.

HE HEARD THE thunderous pounding of hooves approaching in the distance.

The MacLeod had tracked down the Hart wench.

He growled and pulled on the reins of his horse, veering him to the right so they could hide in the shadows of the trees whilst the MacLeod rode by.

The appearance of the laird-to-be meant that he would need to cut down both of them. It wouldn't be easy. It would be harder now that he was joining her.

But he would figure it out.

One way or another, neither the MacLeod nor the Hart bitch would make it out of the highlands.

DAWN WAS CRESTING when Errol got his first glimpse of Moira riding her mare up ahead. He breathed a sigh of relief seeing that she was alone, and no harm had come to her.

Only the tracks of her horse could be seen on the trail. Mayhap it was only a coincidence that someone else was riding on the same route as she was earlier. Whoever it was, they were no longer here.

He slowed his horse, so the sound of its pounding hooves didn't startle Moira and cause her to topple off her mount.

As he neared, he noticed Moira's back stiffen. She heard him approaching. She didn't look back, but he did watch as she leaned forward to scratch her leg, at least that was what she wanted the casual onlooker to see. He kenned better. He'd seen that move afore.

She wrapped her fingers around the hilt of her small dagger and brought it up with her, hiding it along the inseam of her arm.

Since she was aware he was there. That someone was there, he thought it best he call out to her. That way she wasn't frightened and could set herself at ease.

"Moira," he called out, his voice loud enough for her to hear, but not so loud that it would startle her.

Her head turned slightly to the left. Was she trying to see him out of the corner of her eye?

"Moira," he called again. "Halt."

She straightened her spine, sitting up straighter in her saddle. "Ye shouldnae have followed me," she snapped, making no move to slow or stop.

"Ye were foolish to leave. Do ye ken what type of danger ye put yerself in?" He hadn't meant to be so blunt, but he could not help it. Her choice to leave could have brought her great harm.

Her horse stopped and she spun it around to face him. "Ye have no right to tell me what I should or shouldnae be doing, Errol MacLeod. Ye lost that privilege when ye turned me away. Shunned me, in essence."

"'Twas no' like that."

"No? Ye pushed me away. Said I meant naught to ye."

She swiped at a tear that spilled down her cheek.

He felt like an arse. He was a bastard. What seemed like the right approach when he didn't ken how it affected her was much easier when he didn't see her cry. Her tears were like a fist to his gut.

"Will ye stop? Please."

"I am taking yer advice and attempting to finish this quest so that we may return to our respective homes. Ye said it yerself. 'Tis the only way to move forward," she said with a sniffle.

"Moira." His voice was low.

She looked at him, her gaze boring into his. His heart broke at the unshed tears glistening in her eyes.

He'd done that to her.

"If ye stop, I can explain."

A flock of birds took flight, startling them both. His eyes snapped to the area, scanning the thick canopy of trees. He didn't see aught suspicious and turned his attention back to Moira.

"I beg of ye, Lass. Please."

She rolled her bottom lip between her teeth as she slowed her horse. Looking up at the sky, he could see that she was conflicted. Her mare stopped and he stopped Dubh Bàn beside her, dismounting and approaching Moira.

"Have ye been riding all this time or have ye stopped to rest?"

Swinging her leg over she slid down, but when her feet touched the ground, her legs gave away.

Quickly, he moved to catch her so she didn't fall.

"I have got ye," he said warmly, cradling her to him, reveling in the feel of her in his arms.

She made no move to push him away and he smiled, saying a silent prayer of thanks. If she didn't pull away, mayhap she was thinking about giving him a chance to explain himself. He was hopeful that she would.

Remaining stiff in his arms, she didn't say a word.

He didn't mind. He was content holding her as close as she would allow.

After a few long moments, he looked down at her. "Do ye think ye can stand on yer own?"

Nodding, she peeled away from him and took a step back.

A fallen log provided the perfect place for them to sit and talk and he pointed to it in offering.

Her lips pinched together, she clasped her hand in front of her and made her way to the log, dropping down and taking a seat. Folding her hands in her lap, she waited for him to join her.

When he did, she straightened her legs in front of her, saying naught.

Sitting so close to her, Errol could feel the heat emanating off her body, seeping into his arm that touched hers. "I am sorry."

Moira snapped her eyes to his. "For what do ye apologize for?"

He sighed. Of course, she would want him to say everything aloud. "For pushing ye away."

"Pfft. Ye are no' the first man to do that to me. I am for certs ye willnae be the last."

That last statement made him angry. She was acting as if there would be someone else after him. As if she would return to Hartsmoor and find someone else to capture her heart.

Over his dead body.

He blew out an exasperated breath. "If I am being honest, truly honest, I must admit that I am scared." There. He'd said it. He refused to look at her face. He didn't want to see the way she would look at him once she learned he was less than a man. Men don't get scared. Not men like him. He was a warrior. Made for battle. "I feel like a coward for no' admitting to my true feelings.

This," he pointed his index finger between the two of them. "Whate'er this is that we have happening betwixt us, 'tis something that we have been told our whole lives that it cannae be." He wet his dry lips afore continuing.

"I am conflicted betwixt following my heart and completing my duty to the clan. Duty that has been hammered into my head since the day I was born."

"I can understand that," she said quietly.

Her statement surprised him.

"But just because ye understand it, doesnae make it right. When we kissed," he turned to her, taking hold of her tiny hand in his. "I felt those kisses with the whole of my being. A feeling I have ne'er experienced afore. It scared me."

"Did ye like our kisses?" Her voice was quiet, small, and filled with uncertainty. He hated that he was the one that was the cause of her pain. He hated that in his decision to protect her by pushing her away, he had instead pushed her into danger.

"Och, aye, Lass. I liked them verra much. Mayhap, too much. It caused all these new emotions that I have ne'er had to deal with afore. I could hear my da's voice in my head, continuously saying 'she's a Hart. She's a Hart.' And that goes against all that I have been taught."

"But we have uncovered documents that show that we shouldnae be enemies. That at one time we were joined and that we can be joined again. Dinnae ye want that?"

"I do. But there are so many barriers we need to break through."

"Tell me one."

Errol studied Moira's face. Her big, blue eyes that reminded him of the sea in the middle of summer, wild and bright. Her pale skin that she protected from the sun. Her thick, dark blonde hair that she'd plaited and hung over her shoulder. She was the most beautiful woman he'd ever seen. It pained him to think that if they couldn't overcome the obstacles that stood in their way that he would need to let her go.

And that revelation scared him more than aught else.

CHAPTER EIGHTEEN

MOIRA WATCHED AS a myriad of emotions flickered across Errol's handsome face as she waited for him to answer her question.

Aye, they had barriers to overcome. But she felt if they talked about them, they could come up with a resolution that would satisfy them both.

Satisfy both of their clans.

Because the other option was them returning to their lives as they were afore, and she wasn't willing to do that. She didn't think it was possible. Not after the time they'd spent together. Her insides felt hollow at the thought of not spending the rest of her days with Errol. Family differences be damned. Why couldn't they show the items they'd found to their families and explain how everything they had kenned had been built upon a lie? They needed to bring the clan that was at the root of all of this death and fighting to justice. They should pay for all they've done throughout the years.

"The death of Gavin, my brother," Errol finally said, his voice barely above a whisper as he squeezed his eyes shut.

The breeze picked up and loosened wisps of her hair from her plait, tickling her nose. She tucked the loose strands behind her ear. "We have talked about it a little. Tell me about what happened." He had told her some of the facts surrounding his brother's death, but not everything. It was important that she learned of all that happened that fateful day.

Patiently, she waited, understanding that it wasn't an easy topic for him to speak about.

"As I said previously, he was traveling with a few MacLeod warriors, visiting the kirkyard that we searched for clues. Unlike us, my brother and his men were there to pay respect to those that perished long ago. It was something that we always did when in that area." He paused, his eyes staring off into the distance, and Moira kenned he was thinking about that day. "It had to have been an ambush. Men lying in wait kenning they would be passing through. My brother was an excellent tracker. He was younger than I, but he kenned this land well. He had a keen sense of the sounds around him. 'Tis why I think the attackers were already here. Gavin no doubt would have heard them if they followed them on their journey. And he wouldnae have let men trail them unchallenged. As Gavin and his men kneeled in front of the graves of our ancestors, praying for their souls, they were attacked. Struck down." He blew out a steadying breath, flattening his palms on his trews.

"When they hadnae returned when they should have, we gave them a bit of time, but soon, we kenned something was amiss. Gavin ne'er missed a return time. I rode out with some of my own warriors and found the slain men."

Pain pierced Moira's heart. She couldn't fathom the pain of such a loss. The abject horror he must have felt at finding his brother in such a way. "I am verra sorry, Errol. I cannae imagine what that must have been like for ye."

"'Twas the Harts that had done it. They killed the whole party."

Moira frowned, shaking her head. "That doesnae make any sense. My da would ne'er order such a senseless attack. I would have heard something. No' only that, it happened on MacLeod lands. Deep into MacLeod lands, no less. We stay off yer lands. 'Tis our way to keep the peace as best we can."

"No' that day."

"Why do ye believe 'twas us?"

"The Hart colors were tucked into my brother's belt. No one else would do that."

She chewed on her lip, thinking about what he had just said. "Errol, if we were trying to keep the peace and avoid war, which is what we have been doing for years, why would we do such a thing that would only guarantee a war betwixt us?"

Errol shrugged. "Men do stupid things. With so many years of strife 'tis only natural that war would erupt at some point."

She nodded. "Aye, I understand that. Howe'er, no war was called from either side. Doesnae that mean that neither side could prove who was behind the attack. Surely, yer father would have declared war if he kenned for certs that we were the ones to strike down yer brother. I dinnae ken him well and havenae spent any surmountable time with him, but he doesnae strike me as the type of man to hold back on such a miscarriage of justice if he could prove it. Especially since it was his son."

Tilting his head to the side, Errol squinted his eyes as he stared into the trees.

Moira kenned he wasn't seeing the trees. Instead, he was picturing the scene from that day. Re-enacting what he believed to have happened.

"What if someone was trying to frame us for the attack, hoping that 'twould cause yer clan to retaliate? In doing so, a clan war would ensue. Who would benefit from that?"

"I dinnae believe that is a scenario we had thought about. With the Hart colors left behind, we believed it was a message to show what ye were capable of."

"We wouldnae do that." She sat straighter, pushing him on her earlier thought. "Why then, also, didnae yer father attack? If he truly thought 'twas us, and he had our colors left on yer brother's body, why wouldnae he have declared war on us and attacked? Does yer father believe something else had happened?"

Errol looked as if he were thinking about what she had suggested. He scrubbed his face with his hands. "Ye are right. It doesnae make sense. But why, then would my father still insist we remain enemies?"

"I do no' ken. Did he have aught to gain by doing so?" She hated to ask the question. It seemed like she was placing blame on his father, but that wasn't what she was trying to do at all. She only wanted to get to the bottom of the mystery surrounding Gavin's death because it seemed like the biggest obstacle they needed to overcome. If it was proven that her clan had killed Gavin and his men, then she and Errol didn't have a chance at a future together, no matter how strong their feelings.

"It may be a discussion I need to have with my da when I return home." He nudged her shoulder. "After we finish this quest. Forgive me?"

She chewed the inside of her cheek as she contemplated whether or not she should. "Ye really hurt me." It pained her to admit it, but if she was going to forgive him then he needed to ken the consequences his actions had. "I dinnae e'er want to feel that way again."

He nodded, sucking his top lip between his teeth. "I understand and I am verra sorry. If it helps, I hated pushing ye away when all I wanted to do was wrap ye in my arms."

Moira met his gaze, searching for Errol's eyes for any sort of deception, but she found none. "Do ye still?" She asked, her voice barely above a whisper. Her breath caught in her throat as she waited anxiously for his answer.

"I do. Verra much."

Smiling, she couldn't stop the elation she felt at his confession.

"Then I suggest we carry on so we can find this supposed treasure and start healing the rift betwixt our families."

"But first," Errol said afore drawing her into his strong arms and capturing her mouth in a passionate kiss that had her toes curling and left her wanting more. He fists clutched as his tunic and she pulled him closer. She didn't want any space betwixt them. The fire he stoked within her building and building.

This man held her heart in his hands. She loved him. That was the all-consuming feeling she felt whenever she thought about him. But she kept those three little words that held such big meaning to herself. She wasn't sure if Errol was ready to hear them and the last thing she wanted to do was scare him away when he was just finally starting to admit to himself that they could have a future together—if they could solve the mysteries they'd uncovered.

THEY RODE ON, side by side, stealing glances at each other, smiling shyly when their eyes met. When they arrived at the coast, Moira paused and took in the beautiful sight. The deep blue water looked crisp and cool, the waves lapping gently against the shore. A pebbly beach beckoned her to strip off her boots and stick her toes in the earth.

She was tempted to do just that as she dismounted and walked to the water. Errol came up behind her, wrapping his arms around her waist as he nuzzled her neck. She leaned her head to the side to give him better access as she brought her arm up to caress the back of his neck.

Heaven. That's where they were. Out here, with no one else around, it was as if all was perfect in the world.

Errol placed a soft kiss on her neck, and she shivered on a sigh. She really wanted more as that heat in her belly grew into an aching she didn't quite understand.

Turning in his arms, she tipped her head up to his. His chin was scruffy with beard-growth, and she ran her fingers along the stubble, feeling the roughness under her fingertips.

Soft brown eyes, crinkling at the corners, met hers. "I want to kiss ye, Moira Hart."

"Well, then, what are ye waiting for Errol MacLeod?"

The searing kiss that followed left Moira weak in the knees. She was thankful for the strong arms Errol wrapped around her. They kept her balanced and standing when all she wanted to do was swoon and drop into a puddle as his tongue delved into her mouth, finding hers and sliding along it.

Sigh.

This man would be the death of her.

Breaking the kiss, Errol leaned his forehead upon hers. "Lass, the things ye make me want to do to ye," he confessed.

She looked at him expectantly, without any idea of what he spoke of. When he didn't say aught further, she asked, "What things?"

He chuckled. "Things I cannae say aloud else ye think I'm a heathen."

His statement only confused her more. "I dinnae believe that. I couldna. E'er."

"That is a discussion for another time." He clasped her hand in his. "Come, let us go to the hollow."

Her pulse quickened. They were here. She figured they were close but wasn't sure how close they were. Letting Errol lead the way, she followed him off the pebble beach and toward the tree line. They entered the darkness of the trees, so tall and thick they blocked all of the sun's rays from filtering through.

"Is it far?" She asked, her excitement growing.

"Nay. We are almost there." His eyes were shiny with excitement of what they would uncover.

Would it be another clue sending them to another location? Or had they finally reached their final destination?

The trees parted to an open space. Wildflowers bloomed under the filtering rays of the sun, their fragrant scent tickling her nose. Tall grass filled the middle. Moira spun around taking it all in.

"This is beautiful," she said in awe.

"Aye." Errol pulled on his neck as he watched her. "'Tis been here for as long as I can remember, but 'tis so far away from e'erything we dinnae come often. But the clue mentioned a hollow and this is the only one I ken of on MacLeod lands."

In the center of the clearing was a huge boulder, its top covered with green and gray moss. Moira walked over and circled it, looking for something that would point to what they needed to do next. Not finding a clue, she moved to the tree line and walked the perimeter.

What if one of the trees held the clue? What if the tree had died? Been cut? These clues had been hidden years and years ago. Things happened over time. There was no guarantee that the clue still existed.

Errol had taken out his dagger and was picking away at the moss that had built up on the boulder over the years, clearing it away.

"What are ye doing?" She asked, sidling up to him and watching him curiously.

He shrugged. "Probably something foolhardy, but I had a thought that mayhap they carved something into the rock? Years ago, it may have been easily read, but now, with the all the moss, ye cannae see it."

"That is a great idea," she said, grabbing her own dagger and starting to do the same.

It was menial, methodical work, but they finally removed the moss from the boulder. Standing back, they both assessed it, searching for a clue. Naught stood out, showing them what they were looking for.

"Well, it indeed looks like that was a foolhardy thing to do. I dinnae see aught," Errol said, tucking his dagger away.

Moira walked around the rock, studying the spots they'd removed the moss from when the smallest of carvings, barely visible, caught her eye.

"Errol, look." When he approached, she pointed to a small arrow notched into the boulder. It pointed to the left of them, where a cluster of trees grew. They followed the direction of the arrow and studied the trees. "This one," Moira tapped her finger on a notch in the bark. "And this one." There was another notch, neither natural. "What do ye think this means?"

He looked at the ground. "I think it means we dig."

"With what? The ground looks thickly packed." The ground would be hard to dig through. The earth hadn't been disturbed for years and it was packed with mud, twigs, pine needles, and dead leaves.

Errol searched the forest floor, finding a curved branch, sturdy and sharp enough to pierce through the thick top layer of leaves and pine needles packed tight with mud.

Once that was removed, it was easier to dig through the softer dirt underneath.

On her knees, she used her hands to scoop and remove the dirt, not caring that it was getting crusted under her fingernails. If her mother or sisters saw her now, they would scold her insufferably. Her mother would probably lock her away in her room and never let her come out until she acted like a proper lady.

Across from her, Errol smiled wildly as they continued to dig until their fingers brushed against something solid.

Moira's eyes widened as she quickened her digging. "'Tis another chest. Bigger than the last."

"Aye," Errol agreed, looking at her with a huge grin on his face. "Ye did it, Lass."

She smiled. "Nay, *we* did it, Errol."

It took some time for them to uncover the breadth of the chest. It was much bigger than the smaller one they had found earlier. Their chests were heaving with exertion as they finally finished digging around the intricately carved trunk.

"It looks heavy." Moira wasn't sure how they could lift it from its resting place.

"I believe we will need to open it from there and remove the items inside afore we can lift it out."

She nodded. That made sense. It was too deep to grasp it well and lift it out with it being so heavy.

Errol pointed to the clasp. "Go ahead," he urged. "'Tis yer treasure to uncover. Open the lid."

With her fingers on the latch, she paused, her eyes meeting Errol's once again. "What do ye think is inside."

He shook his head and chuckled. "Naught of what we have found so far was aught that I would have expected, so I cannae e'en guess as to what is inside. Mayhap some more coin. Mayhap some more carved figurines. I dinna ken. But one thing I am for certs is inside."

"What?"

"Another letter."

"Ah," she nodded with a smile. "I bet ye are right." With that, she pulled on the latch, surprised that it gave way and opened without out too much resistance. Lifting the lid, her breath quickened as she revealed a painstakingly embroidered handkerchief. Like the paintings and carvings they had found, the needlepoint also told a story. She lifted it carefully, sitting on the forest floor and spread it out over her lap so she could look at the pictures depicted in the delicate threading.

Instead of multiple scenes like the previous clues they had found, on the handkerchief, in fine gold threading, was one large picture. Once again, the Harts and MacLeods were represented, no longer as one unit, but on their separate sides much like the first painting. Depicted on the side of the MacLeods was a grave with a young lad standing near. The grave had to be for Thomas. The lad Angus. On the land separating the two clans, was a small coffin, which Moira guessed was to depict Agnes. On the Hart side stood Fiona. Alone. Her clan members had their backs turned to her. In essence shunning her.

Moira swiped at a tear that slipped down her cheek. The scene broke her heart. Fiona had lost everything. Her husband. Her daughter. Her son. Her home. Even her clan. Moira couldn't imagine the pain she went through. The poor woman had no one to lean on and offer a kind gesture.

In the right-hand corner, there was one final picture sewn

with red thread. The cliffs they'd ridden to were there, and a woman, which had to be Fiona, was falling through the air, halfway between the cliffs and rocky water below.

Moira gasped, as she brought her hand to her mouth, horror at the realization of what the picture meant.

Errol moved to her side, wrapping his arms around her shoulders. "What is it?"

She met his gaze. His brows were drawn down in concern. "'Tis Fiona. She jumped from the cliffs."

◆—————————————◆

CHAPTER NINETEEN

MOIRA'S FACE WAS stricken with what they had unveiled. She had grown quite close to Fiona over their journey even though she'd never met the woman. Errol could understand. The trials and tribulations the woman had gone through in her young life, depicted throughout the items they'd uncovered, was more than anyone should have to experience.

Multiple times, Moira had stated she did not want to read on to discover whatever tragic ending the family had met. Kenning they needed to continue hadn't changed her mind.

But with that knowledge, neither of them could have guessed the horrors the family had endured.

He held her while she sobbed into his tunic, wetting the linen with her tears. Distraught for the endured tragedy of a woman she had never met. Her heart was huge and welcoming. Her capacity to love was unending.

Stroking her back with gentle swipes of his hand, Errol let Moira cry until she had no more tears and she pushed away from him, sniffling.

"She deserved so much more. They all did."

"Aye." He tipped her chin to him so he could look in her eyes. "'Tis why we are here. To right the wrongs that were done to them." This time, when Errol said, he believed it. The journey wasn't about the treasure. It was about fixing the past and mending the rift betwixt the clans.

She nodded. Biting her lip. "Thank ye."

Confusion overcame him. "For what?"

"Letting me have a cry. I ken 'tis no' something ye fancy—having a women cry all over ye."

He drew her close and hugged her tightly. "Ye can cry on me any time ye need to, Lass."

They sat that way for a long time. Both lost in their own thoughts.

Finally, Moira said, "I suppose we should go through the rest of the items in the chest. Mayhap we will learn the full story."

He nodded, letting her pull away from him, even though every bone in his body screamed to pull her back against him.

She crawled over to the hole they had dug, not a care for the dirt that was staining her skirts as she did so. Errol admired that about her. She wasn't afraid to get dirty. Reaching down into the chest, she pulled out an item wrapped in linen. Unwinding the item from its covering, Moira revealed a dagger with a jewel encrusted handle. The hilt was made of gold and looked more ceremonial than practical, though it would cause damage if the situation appraised itself. But it looked more like a dagger one would wear during an official ceremony to show his station and standing within a clan. At the size of the emerald and ruby on either side of the handle, whoever owned this dagger must have been wealthy. And important.

"'Tis beautiful," Moira whispered, carefully lying it on its former linen covering and dug back into the chest with fervor.

She withdrew a small satchel, jingling it in the air afore looking inside. "It sounds like coins."

Errol nodded in agreement.

She pulled the strings tied into a cinch and let the bag fall open. Silver and gold winked at them from the opening, and she set it to the side.

She reached in again and came back with two matching rings. "Do ye think these were Fiona and Thomas's marital rings?"

It wasn't common for both the husband and wife to wear a ring, but it looked like the two were a matched pair. "Could be."

Squinting, Moira looked closer at the rings. "Each one is engraved with the same stag and lion creature we found earlier."

"Then I would say they are definitely their marital rings."

She peered down into the chest again. "This next item appears to be large."

"Do ye need assistance retrieving it?" He asked, not wanting to overstep. This was still her quest and he wanted to ensure he didn't trample over her boundaries.

Shaking her head, she reached down, biting her lip in concentration as she pulled and tugged at the object. After a few minutes, she brought the item out.

Both of them just stared at what had been uncovered. The bold meaning and strong symbolism behind it.

In Moira's hands was a coat of arms. Half Hart, half MacLeod. It included the stag lion hybrid they had now become familiar with. The arms blended both of their clan's coats of arms together perfectly.

True unison.

"'Tis amazing." Moira said in awe and gestured to the coat of arms. "'Tis the proof we need to show our families that we were once one." Her bright eyes, alit with newfound hope, clashed with his.

Errol nodded, if only it were that easy though. Their families would need much more to end the feuding. They would expect much more to erase the years and years of fighting. The lives lost. The men, women, and children injured in the name of a war that they didn't ken the cause of.

Moira reached back into the chest. Also included inside were squares of the Hart and MacLeod plaids, sewn together to combine and create new colors for a united clan.

"All of these things can be used to show our families what we've discovered." Moira turned to Errol. "To show them that we can be together." She looked at him timidly. "If that is what ye want, of course. I understand if 'tis no'. I have a way of scaring people away. I am too forward. To undisciplined. I dinnae listen—"

Errol captured her lips in his, cutting off her rambling and smiled against her mouth. Her arms looped around his neck as she kissed him back with a sigh, her body relaxing into his. It was the best feeling. One he had never experienced afore. His reaction told him that what he and Moira were experiencing was real. That she was the one for him.

The only one.

"I will gladly accept yer undisciplined self, lass. Ne'er change. Whoe'er 'twas that told ye to change those things about yerself were daft. I wouldnae change a thing when it comes to ye."

Her blue eyes rounded afore crinkling with her wide smile. His groin tightened. Lord above, he wanted this woman. He wanted to watch as her eyes blew wide with passion as he brought her to depths she never kenned existed.

But not here. He wouldnae disrespect her by taking her here on the dirty forest floor. Nay, she deserved to have her body worshipped in a warm, soft bed. But, later, after they had learned every inch of each other's body, an evening spent under the stars, loving her long and slow in the way she deserved, would be divine.

"How is it that ye can understand me so, when my own family cannae?"

He shrugged. "I dinna ken. Mayhap they are worried about their own concerns. Yer brothers, well, that should be obvious. They're men."

"As are ye," she countered.

"Aye. But I will swear on my life that yer brothers are not looking at ye the way I am. That would be sinful."

Moira gasped, her cheeks flaming red. "Errol MacLeod!"

With a lift of his shoulders, he grinned. "I speak only the truth." He dipped his head to the hole where the chest was. "Is there aught else in there?"

She peered into the hole and nodded. "A letter. Just as we expected." She reached in and carefully withdrew the letter. Folded into a square and tied with twine. Gently, she tugged at the bow tying the bundle together and it fell away.

She clasped the letter to her chest, near her heart, and took a deep breath, sighing. "Are we ready for this? For certs, this is the last one. I cannae imagine there is aught else for us to discover."

He nodded. "I believe ye are right." He stood, holding out his hand for Moira to accept.

She looked up at him with question in her eyes.

"Let us go out into the clearing and let the sun warm our skin as ye read the letter."

Her gaze dropped to the items she'd removed from the chest.

"Dinnae fash, lass. They will be here when we finish and return. There is no one else here."

Biting her lip, she nodded, accepting his hand and he pulled her up.

Outside of the cool shade of the trees, the sun felt refreshing. Nourishing. Chasing away the darkness of the past.

Errol led her to the boulder that started their hollow quest and dropped to the ground, drawing Moira down to his side, his arm around her shoulders. His fingers drew slow circles against her arm as he waited for her to unfold the letter and start reading.

CHAPTER TWENTY

MOIRA FELT AS if she were dreaming. Together she and Errol had completed what they set out to do—find the treasure.

The final piece she held tightly in her hands. She blew out a breath. What could the letter possibly say? They had already uncovered the tragic ending to the love story of Thomas and Fiona. Sadness covered her like a blanket at the thought of the young family that had been devastated by the actions of a sick, selfish bastard. What else could the letter tell them?

There was only one way to find out.

Slowly, carefully, she unfolded the square, the parchment old, frayed in the creases where it had been folded for years.

'Thank ye. First and foremost, that is what I must say to ye, the one who fought to get to the end and uncover the truth. Ye have accomplished what I could not. I tried. Believe me when I say that. But I could not overcome the ire both families set upon my shoulders. Ye have found the final chest and therefore ye ken what my next steps are. Once I bury this final chest, I will walk upon the cliffs and join my dear husband, Thomas, and our darling daughter, Agnes, in eternity. I pray that the MacLeod treat Angus as their own and that he grows to be braw like his da. I have not seen him since my shunning from both clans. I can only hope that they tell him about his da one day. I hope he learns how much he was loved. I ken that I will not be part of *that conversation. A part of those memories. I am no' happy about it, but I have resigned myself to that truth. As to our beautiful daughter's killer, it was the MacPhail. It was he who was infatuated with her. Did those awful things to her. When Thomas confronted him, MacPhail and his brothers attacked. 'Twas too much for Thomas to defend himself against. It was also the MacPhail that went to the MacLeod, painting a story that I killed my daughter and my husband and in doing so set in motion a feud to last, well, I do not ken, but I am sure a long time. When ye find this, I pray that the feud has ended, and the clans have reconciled. If not, then please, let the items ye have found finally put an end to all the fighting that for certs has happened. And finally, my wish is that the MacPhail pay for all they have done. All the pain they have caused. They should pay.*

Fiona M.'

Moira looked at Errol and couldn't stop the tears that once again flowed down her cheeks. She swiped at them angrily. She was both sad and furious. Sad for all that happened to Fiona and her family and angry at the senseless cause of it all.

"The MacPhail," she started. "Arenae they the clan that held a small parcel of land betwixt our lands?" She gasped. "Is that the land that was given to Thomas and Fiona? Did they no' only take the lives of Agnes and Thomas, and Fiona in a sense," she added. "But they also took their land?"

Errol frowned, as he rubbed the stubble on his chin. "I believe ye may be correct. I havenae seen them for quite some time. I will have to ask my father if he kens, but I believe they moved on. Naught has been done on the land. But it must be the land Fiona spoke about. I ken of no other that would fit."

The sharp crack of a branch breaking in the nearby woods caught their attention. Moira sat up quickly, her eyes scanning the woods as Errol stood straight, his hand going to the hilt of the sword at his side.

"What is it?" Moira asked nervously, fear settling deep into her bones.

"Could be just an animal."

"Or?" She wasn't sure she wanted to ken the answer, even though she kenned what the other possibility was.

Had more bandits tracked them down?

Would they attack them once again? Were they in the woods now collecting the items that she and Errol had pulled from the final chest?

"The artifacts," she said with worry.

"Stay near me." Errol's voice was low, but strong and steady, his eyes searching the woods. It was so dark once you passed the line of the trees, it was impossible to see deep into the forest. Ten men could be watching them. Mayhap even more, and they would not be able to tell because they couldn't see them.

Moira withdrew her dagger. "The blade from the chest. What if they have taken it?"

Errol shook his head. "I wouldnae fash about that just yet. If someone has come and they are here for the treasure, 'twill be there after they dispatch us."

Moira gasped. "We are going to die? Nay." She refused to end up like Thomas and Fiona.

"I didnae say that. Stay calm. I am just saying that that is more than likely their plan, whoe'er 'tis. 'Twould be easier to gather up the treasure if there was no one preventing them from doing so. Naught will happen to ye, Lass. I promise ye."

A whir in the air sounded and Errol pushed her to the ground. "Christ!" He swore as he lifted his head in the direction the arrow came from. He took a deep breath. "An archer. And we are sitting out in the open. We can move to the other side, but if there are multiple archers, they will have all sides covered."

Moira's heart sped up, her blood pounding in her ears as her eyes searched the trees frantically. She didn't want to die at the end of an arrow. Or any other way for that matter. Nay, she wanted to live and bring Thomas and Fiona's story to light. To solve the rift betwixt their two clans and move forward in peace and unification.

"I dinnae believe 'tis an experienced archer. We were sitting still, and yet he missed."

"What if 'twas just a warning arrow? What if the next one pierces one of our hearts."

He took her by the shoulders, dropping his head so he could look her in her eyes. Their gazes locked. "I willnae let that happen. I promise ye, Lass. This is no' how we end."

His stare was so convincing. Confident.

"Understand?" He asked, his fingers squeezing.

She nodded.

"All right. We are closest to the woods behind us. They are our best chance for cover. At my command, I want ye to run to them, fast as ye can."

Was he daft?

"Nay! 'Tis a sure way to an untimely death."

Errol kissed the top of her head. "Remember, lass. I said no harm will come to ye. I will shield ye."

"So ye can take the arrow, leaving me alone to fend for my-self? Absolutely no'!"

"Moira," Errol drawled, his voice steely. "We cannae stay where we are. We must move."

"I dinnae want to," she said stubbornly, but also out of fear, which made her legs feel heavy. She wasn't sure she would be able to run.

Errol took hold of her shoulders, giving her a slight shake to get her to focus on him. "Look at me. Listen to me. Naught is going to happen to ye."

She started to speak, and he pressed a finger to her lips to quiet her.

"Nay. Listen. To. Me," he said slowly. "This is no' e'en close to the worst situation I have been in. Do ye trust me?"

She darted her tongue out, wetting her suddenly dry lips, and nodded.

"Good. At my word, I want ye to run to that copse of trees o'er there. See them?"

She looked over his shoulder and identified the spot he spoke of, and nodded.

"Good. Run as fast as ye can. Zig zag if ye want, just run quickly. Stay low. The boulder will help shield ye."

"What about ye?" She asked, her lips quivering.

"Dinnae fash about me. I will be right behind ye. Understand?" He bent, staring into her eyes. "Do ye understand?"

Looking over his shoulder into the trees on the far side of the hollow, Moira tried to see whoever was out there, but she couldn't see aught. It was too dark and shadows blended together making the landscape look creepy and foreboding.

"Moira?" Errol asked.

Taking a deep breath, she brought her gaze back to his. "I understand."

He smiled encouragingly. "Ye are a strong woman, Moira Hart. The strongest I ken."

She didn't believe that, but she didn't have the energy to fight with him about it right then.

"Stand up, but stay hunched o'er," he ordered.

Doing as she was told, she waited, staring straight ahead to the destination she needed to run to.

"Now!" Errol urged. "Go, Moira!"

Off she ran, staying low, but pumping her legs as fast as she could. Feeling the burn in her thighs, but she ignored it. Ignored the heavy feel of them trying to slow her down. She couldn't hear Errol behind her. She wanted to turn and make for certs he was there, but she needed to concentrate on not falling. The trees drew closer. An arrow whizzed by her, sinking into the ground to her right.

She screamed and hunched even lower, even though it made her advance clumsy, and pumped her legs harder.

Closer. The trees were right there. Just a few more steps and she would safe. The searing pain that lanced her side felt like fire. She sank to the ground, grasping at her side. She brought her hand up and saw that it was soaked in blood.

Nay.

They were so close. Where was Errol? She couldn't see him, but she couldn't stay where she was. She needed to get into the safety of the trees. Pushing off the ground, she moaned in pain, black spots appeared behind her eyes and she fought through the temptation to fall back on the ground and finally made it to the safety of the trees. At the edge she dropped down into the darkness, her face falling into the pine needles and mud, but she didn't care. She'd made it.

THERE WAS ONLY one archer. That was good for them. Judging from the aim of the arrows so far, the archer wasn't one that was well-seasoned. Nay, Errol believed it was someone that was either very new to the bow and arrow or someone that didn't possess the skill to be a good archer.

Either way, that bode well for them. Whoever it was had loosed several arrows whilst they ran. It was a gamble to not run behind Moira as she headed towards the trees and acted as a shield. One that he would most definitely never tell her about. But he figured since he was the bigger threat, he would draw the arrows to him and allow Moira to get to the cover of the trees safely.

He didn't think she would ever forgive him for doing that and he wouldn't blame her.

APPLYING PRESSURE TO her side to try to stop the bleeding, Moira scanned the trees looking around for Errol. She didn't see him. Her heart quickened. Where was he? Had he been shot by an arrow as well? She frantically searched the ground, looking for his prone body laying lifelessly in the clearing. She heard footsteps behind her and turned best as she could. Her dagger raised as high as she could manage, ready to strike whoever approached.

"Lass, 'tis me." Errol had his hands up.

"I. How? I, I thought ye were behind me?" She wanted to rush into his arms and hug him close. She wanted to cling to him like he was her lifeline and not let him go. But she couldn't even stand. Her energy was quickly ebbing and she fought the temptation to close her eyes.

"I took a different path. There is only one archer. He couldna shoot two places at one time." He knelt beside her and grasped her hand. It was then he noticed her injury, his eyes blowing wide and his forehead creased with concern. "Jesus, Lass." His eyes dropped to her side, looking at the side of her gown which she was for certs was now saturated with her blood. "Nay, nay, nay," he repeated and ripped off his tunic, wrapping it around her waist in an attempt to staunch the flow of blood. "We need to go deeper in the woods and get ye to safety."

She gave him a small smile—it was the biggest one she could muster as she tried to lift her hand to caress his cheek. The effort was too much, and her hand fell limply to her side. "I am safe with ye here, now." Her voice sounded far away.

Scooping her up in arms, Errol was careful not to jostle her overly much and moved further into the darkness of the trees, moving fast but sure-footed. She was cold and couldn't stop the shiver that overtook her body.

"Ye will be fine, Lass." His words were quiet, almost pleading as if he were saying the words to convince himself as much as her. He laid her on the ground gently.

"I am sorry," she said quietly as he pulled away his tunic and assessed the wound in her side.

"Ye need stitches. I need to get to the horses and our supplies."

She clutched at his arms. "Dinnae leave me, Errol. I dinnae want to be alone," she cried, a tear slipping from the corner of her eye. Images of death swam afore her eyes. She didn't want to die.

Not now. Not when she and Errol were so close to mending the strife betwixt their families.

Not afore she told Errol she loved him.

She could tell him now, but her mouth didn't want to move. And her eyes wouldn't remain opened. She was slipping into the fog that threatened to consume her.

"Moira." Her name sounded so far away. As if she were being called from the other side of a long tunnel. "Lass, wake up." Warmth wrapped around her and she welcomed it as the fog overwhelmed her and she slipped into black oblivion.

Chapter Twenty-One

F EAR LIKE ERROL had never experienced afore punched him in the gut.

They were safe under the canopy of trees, but not really. The archer was still out there, and they were vulnerable. Moira couldn't run, Hell. He pushed his hands through his short hair. She couldn't even walk if she wanted to. All the color had drained from her face and her skin had taken on an unhealthy waxy pallor.

He was breathing heavily as he assessed their situation. Moira should be breathing heavily as well from running to safety, but her breaths were shallow. She was losing a lot of blood and he needed to stop it.

Moving quickly, he gathered moss to use as a poultice and dropped beside Moira. Her eyes remained closed as he pulled away the tunic he had wrapped around her waist and studied her wound. The arrow appeared to have gone clean through which was good. It meant he wouldn't have to pull it out or through, which would cause her even more pain. It didn't look like the arrow had hit any of her vital organs, for that he was thankful, but she was still bleeding profusely. Fisting the moss, he packed it against the wound as compact as he could, then he ripped strips of his tunic away and tied them tight around her waist to keep the moss in place and apply pressure. Once he'd tied off the last of four strips, he took what was left of his tunic and covered the strip and knotted it.

Confident that it would suffice until he could get to their supplies so he could stitch Moira's wound closed.

Errol didn't want to leave her side, but there was naught he could do for her right now and he needed to stay vigilant.

The man who shot Moira would need to make his way from his hiding place closer to them. He would be daft to come straight through the hollow so Errol was for certs he was taking the long way and walking the circumference of the hollow and would approach them from what would be their back, but Errol was ready.

The bastard that shot at them? That shot Moira and put her life in danger?

He would be dead afore the day was over. It was a vow Errol looked forward to fulfilling.

But first, Errol would find out what he was doing following them. Threatening them. Trying to strike them down.

He was angry with himself that he got so lost in Moira that he hadn't realized they were being followed. Mayhap it was the same person that had been following Moira afore he had caught up with her.

Where had the man gone to disappear from the path earlier?

Errol didn't ken. But he would get the answers he sought.

It was his fault that Moira lay on the ground, her life in the balance. If she died, if he lost her, he would never forgive himself. He wouldn't be able to live with himself.

A snap in the distance drew Errol's attention. He squinted into the trees, trying to see what was making the noise. There was no way the man shooting at them from the clearing had already made his way around. Also, the noise was so faint. Someone adept at not being discovered was behind them.

He looked to Moira but there was no need to warn her to stay quiet. She wasn't going to make a sound.

Errol waited, muscles tight, his hand on the hilt of his sword.

A familiar whistle sounded. To someone unfamiliar with the sound, they would think it were birdsong. Errol kenned better. Their luck was about to change.

He whistled back and waited.

Moira remained unmoving on the ground at his feet.

With a glimmer of hope, Errol repeated the whistle.

There. Not far from them, the leaves rustled, branches moving as a figure made its way to them. Soon, Robbie stepped through, joining them.

Errol stepped up and grasped his cousin's arm and gave him a small smile.

"Robbie, what are ye doing here?" Errol's voice was low as he asked, relieved to see his cousin.

"Yer da sent me. He kens what ye are doing." His eyes swung to Moira, who remained still, and his eyes rounded. "What has happened? She's injured?" His brows drew down in concern. "Will she live?"

"Aye," he said, and he believed it. He had to. She *would* live. He was demanding that she live. "But she needs stitches and I cannae get to our supplies or our horses. There's an archer." Errol dipped his head to the far side of the hollow. "He was shooting from there. I thought he was a bad shot until he hit Moira. The bastard. He will pay with his life," he spat. "I believe he is skirting the circumference of the clearing to come upon us. Mayhap with newfound confidence since he managed to hit one of his targets."

"My men arenae far from here. We've been following yer trail for some time."

"Thank ye. We obviously can use yer men right about now."

Robbie's mouth was a thin line as he gave a curt nod. "I'll get my men." He moved to leave but stopped and turned. "Dinnae get yerself killed afore I come back."

Errol chuckled. "I havenae yet."

He watched his cousin slip quietly through the woods and returned to Moira. "All will be well, Lass. I promise ye with all my heart. I willnae lose ye now."

DAMN HIM AND his off the mark shooting. Orman MacPhail had used up all his arrows trying to cut the pair down, first whilst they were sitting at the boulder, and then when they had each taken off running—in different directions no less. He had focused on the MacLeod bastard. If he could dispatch him first, the Hart bitch would be easy to deal with. But he was too fast, when Errol had disappeared into the woods, Orman loosed his final arrow, and when he saw the wench crumple to the ground he felt this first tinge of satisfaction he'd had in a very long time. Then he saw her rise and make her way to the woods.

The taste of failure filled his mouth. The MacLeod bastard would be stalking him even fiercer than he was afore he'd cut down the bitch. He heard his father laughing, the sound making his ears ring.

"Ye piece of shite. Believing ye could kill aught with yer arrows. Useless. As always. Naught has changed."

"Shut up." Orman called out to the empty woods surrounding him. But his father's taunting voice continued as he lurched through the woods, his foot dragging like it always did. He couldn't move fast, and he couldn't trust his horse to get him to the other side, so he had to walk. He'd dropped his bow. It served no purpose anymore without any arrows to loose.

He had his sword, though. Well, his father's sword. He had never been gifted one. No' like his brother. Nay, his brother had received a sword made of the finest steel with the most intricate design engraved on the blade. Their father had boasted about it proudly and given it to him in a special ceremony in front of the whole clan. His brother had shown it off with pride whenever he had the chance.

Well, he had no use for it now, did he? Nay, instead, the blade was outside, rusting in the well where Orman had thrown it so he wouldn't have to look upon it ever again.

His father's voice was still in his head. Belittling him. Taunting him.

"Useless. Useless. Useless."

He clamped his hands over his ears. "I told ye to shut up!" He shouted. Birds flew from the trees above him at the sudden noise and he swore. "Shite." If the MacLeod didn't ken where he was afore, he did now. And if he truly had wounded the Hart bitch, then Errol would be out for his blood.

Orman paused, waiting to see if Errol would pop out of the trees and attack. When he saw no movement, he continued on. Mayhap the bastard hadn't been alerted to his location.

They had found all the clues. Uncovered the true reason behind the feud betwixt the MacLeods and Harts. Learned that it was naught that they had done, but a contrived plan by the MacPhail.

All that they had found was left at the last treasure they had uncovered. He'd looked through it all whilst they were sitting at the boulder. Then he had listened while the Hart bitch read the contents of the final letter.

He only needed to get rid of them and then he could destroy the clues.

None would be the wiser.

His family's secret would remain just that.

The feuding betwixt the MacLeods and the Harts would continue.

With everything destroyed, there would be no possibility of it ever being uncovered.

All would be right in his world.

So, when he felt the sting of a blade at his back, he was taken by surprise, and his world came crashing down upon him.

ERROL PRESSED THE tip of his sword into the back of the man he had caught shuffling through the woods. How Errol had not heard the louse afore he had no idea, but he was reconsidering his tracking skills. The bastard was so loud, Errol didn't have to make a move to cover the sound of his own footsteps.

A few of Robbie's men, all MacLeod warriors, were protecting Moira, and Robbie and he had taken to the woods in the hopes of catching whoever it was that tried to kill them. He had been torn on leaving Moira or taking chase. But he kenned that he needed to be the one to find the man responsible for wounding Moira. She was in good hands with Robbie's men and one of them was tending to her now, stitching her wound, and making her as comfortable as possible. She had awakened moments afore he left to track down the archer, who, now that Errol could see him, was no archer at all.

Errol promised her he would return soon, and that all would be well. She cupped his face with a weak hand and he placed a gentle kiss on her lips. She was pained, but strong. He could see the light of fire in her eyes and that was what spurred him on to leave her side. He kenned she would be well.

He couldn't say the same for the man at the end of his blade.

The chase was much easier than Errol expected. He would be lying if he wasn't feeling a wee bit disappointed on missing out on a good chase. Though it was better this way. It meant he could soon return to Moira's side. Something he was eager to do.

There was no real chase to be had with this cretin. The man could barely walk, never mind run. It had to have been pure luck that the bastard had managed to hit Moira with one of his loosed arrows.

Errol shoved his sword further into the man's back. "Walk. Now." He ordered as Robbie stepped up and confiscated the man's sword that he had been dragging on the ground.

The bastard spat on the ground, near Robbie's feet.

Errol shot a look to Robbie when he noticed his clenched fist and gave a slight shake of his head. The time would come when the bastard would meet his comeuppance, but they needed answers first.

When they arrived back to where Moira and the warriors waited, Errol was relieved to see that Moira was sitting up, her back against a tree. Their gazes met and she gave him a small smile. She must have seen the question in his eyes, because she nodded, letting him ken she was well. He would be by her side soon and he couldn't wait to gather her in his arms, but he needed to tend to this matter first.

Errol shoved the man to his knees and came around to face him, his sword never leaving the bastard's body.

Moira was wide-eyed as she watched the scene unfold. He should have one of the guards take her to another location, so she didn't have to witness what was inevitably going to be the bastard's demise. There was no other ending. He tried to kill the MacLeod's son. His first-born son. Worse than that, he also tried to kill the Hart's daughter, shot her with an arrow. The man was dead no matter what.

His gaze locked with Moira's. "Do ye wish to leave, Lass?"

Her eyes bounced from Errol's to the man on his knees and then back again. She straightened as best she could without causing too much pain, and pushed her shoulders back, raising her chin defiantly. "I dinnae," she said, her voice steady and strong and a wave of pride washed over Errol. He smiled proudly afore focusing his attention back on the bastard in front of him.

"Yer name?" Errol demanded.

The man seethed as he knelt on the ground, his eyes boring into Errol, but remained quiet, his teeth clenched behind a sneer.

"Ye are already sentenced to death for yer actions earlier. Ye might as well give me the information I seek afore that happens."

His face pinched, and his eyes narrowed, but he finally answered. "MacPhail. Orman MacPhail."

Robbie frowned. "I thought the MacPhail fled their lands. Havenae they been abandoned?"

MacPhail's eyes settled on Robbie. "I still remain."

"What of yer father?" Errol asked.

The bastard's face broke out into an evil grin, and Errol

fought his disgust at the rotting teeth revealed. "Dead."

"The first son?"

His garish grin grew wider. "Also dead. I am the only Mac-Phail left."

"What happened to them?" Errol asked suspiciously.

MacPhail licked his lips and shrugged. "It appears a series of unfortunate accidents has plagued MacPhail lands."

"Ye killed them? Yer own father and brother?"

Errol tried to remember the last time he had seen either man. It had been years. The whole family was reclusive. They stuck to themselves, staying out of other clan's affairs, though Errol now realized why, that is if they were aware of what their ancestors had done.

The bastard's face reddened as he clenched his fists. "They deserved it."

Errol dropped the point of his sword to the forest floor. The bastard was no threat. No' without his sword, which also hadn't posed a threat. He couldn't say the same for his arrows. He'd had many bad shots that Errol would, in most circumstances, not find him a threat in that medium either, but he had managed to hit his target once, and that was more than enough.

"Yer family killed a Hart and a MacLeod. Started a war. Why?"

He laughed evilly. "'Twas years ago. Long afore ye and I or e'en our fathers were born. Afore our grandfathers and those afore them. We have kept the family secret all this time. Until ye uncovered the clues that told the history. We kenned they were out there somewhere, but didnae ken where."

"But why?" Errol growled, frustration boiling through his veins.

"The answers are the oldest kenned to man. Why do we always do the things we do? Coin, land, holdings." He paused, his eyes shooting to Moira and then back to Errol. "Love," he spat.

Moira pushed to a stand, pain etched on her face. Errol moved toward and she shook her head as she approached Orman, disgust prevalent on her face. "Love. Love?" She shouted, her voice so strong is surprised Errol. Her anger was fueling her actions. "Agnes was but a wee lass. 'Twasnae love. 'Twas a disgusting action by a disgusting bastard with no morals." Afore Errol could comprehend what was happening, she pulled her fist back and slammed it into MacPhail's nose. His head snapped back as blood poured from his nostrils. The sick bastard smiled and licked at the drops, staining his teeth red.

"Ouch!" She cried, shaking her fist and grabbing her side with her other hand.

Errol raised his brow at her, surprised and proud of her. "Are ye well?" He asked, concern consuming him.

She opened her fist and wiggled her fingers. "That hurt. But 'twas worth it," she grinned.

He thinks he might love this woman.

Robbie cleared his throat and Errol dropped his smile, focusing back on the man in front of him.

"The MacPhail land, was that the land granted to the MacLeod after he wed the Hart?"

"What do ye think?"

Errol shook his head. But why? It made no sense to keep the fighting going on for so long. "Why keep the clans warring?"

"Do ye no' see? With ye fighting, ye left us alone. We could do what we wanted. Steal what we wanted. *Kill* who we wanted. And ye blamed each other whilst we sat back and watched it continue, keeping our secret safe. Keeping our land."

Something that he said caught Errol's attention. *'Kill who we wanted.'*

Gavin.

Could it have been the MacPhail? The possibility never crossed their minds. The clan had never been thought about for any of the crimes that had been blamed on the Hart. He would lay coin down that if he asked the question to the Hart, they would answer the same.

His voice low, he asked, "What do ye mean, kill who ye

wanted?"

That garish grin appeared once again. "Do ye really think the Harts would be so stupid as to kill a MacLeod son?"

All the emotions that Errol had held inside regarding his brother's killing. The sorrow of his father and sister. The blame and fury they had thrust upon the Harts. All the deaths. The needless deaths. The attempt to take Moira's life. It all came bubbling to the surface in a fierce inferno. Errol dropped his blade to the ground and tackled the bastard that, along with his family, for years and years, had lived without consequences for all they had done. His fist met with flesh as he punched over and over again. Fists flying, the man stopped fighting after the third punch, but Errol couldn't stop. He continued until Robbie and one of his men pulled him off.

Chest heaving, he looked at Orman MacPhail's lifeless body lying on the ground. He flexed his fingers, his knuckles split and bleeding, or was that Orman's blood? It mattered naught. The man was dead. Finally suffering the consequence of all the damage the MacPhail's had done to both families.

Moira was right there, wrapping her arms around him. Comforting him as he was overcome with emotions. He held on to her, gentle so he didn't squeeze her too hard and cause her any more pain, not caring that Robbie and his men saw.

They'd solved the mystery of why the Harts and MacLeods were supposed enemies. They'd found the treasure they sought.

But they'd found something more important than that. More significant. Something that would truly change their lives.

They'd found love.

"I love ye, Lass."

Moira squeezed him tighter.

"I love ye, too, Errol MacLeod. Now, let's go home."

CHAPTER TWENTY-TWO

THAT NIGHT, THEY stopped in a village, one different than they had spent the night afore, and this time, there was no awkwardness when Errol booked one room with one bed, making sure it was big enough for two. No trepidation.

Robbie and his men had gathered the items they'd uncovered, bundled them up and headed back to MacLeod Keep. He would give the items to Errol's father, but not give the details he'd learned. He'd also warned Errol that his father wasn't happy when he had learned of what Errol and Moira were doing, but that it was something that Errol would have to deal with upon his return.

They would explain everything together. The story of their families entwined history would come from she and Errol. She was nervous, but no longer scared.

The innkeeper recognized Errol when he walked in the door of the inn, his eyes widening at the blood splatter on his clothes. "My laird." He'd rushed forward, bowing. "Are ye well?" He turned to Moira and noticed the blood on her, too, and asked the same of her.

She had smiled because the innkeeper didn't look at her with disgust in his eyes. Only with concern.

Errol brought his arm around Moira's shoulders and pulled her closer.

"We are well, thank ye. But we need a room for the night. A hot bath and food."

The innkeeper nodded emphatically. "Right away, my laird. Right away." He snatched a black iron key from a hook behind him and came out from behind the counter, heading for the stairs. Waving his hand, he said, "Follow me. Right this way." He led them to the second floor and down a hall. At the very last room, he pushed the key into the lock and shoved open the door. "This is our most private room, my laird. The largest as well. No one will bother ye here. I shall have a bath brought to ye straightaway, along with provisions. A hot meal as well, unless ye would like to sup in the dining room?"

Errol shook his head. "Nay, we would prefer to sup in our room, but we thank ye for yer generosity."

The man smiled and gave a kenning wink. Moira wasn't sure what that meant, but the man kept bobbing his head up and down as he said, "Right, right. The maids will be up shortly with all ye require. If ye should need aught else, please let me ken."

He left swiftly, closing the door behind him. Moira clasped her hands together, looking around the room and moved toward the roaring fire, she suddenly felt the chill in the air. Her side was sore and tight feeling, and she didn't want to think about how close Orman MacPhail had come to ending her life. The warrior that stitched her wound closed said she was very lucky. No vital organs had been hit and the arrow went straight through. She was thankful for that. It had bled profusely, but he had said that was just the nature of that type of wound, and wasn't the cause of her slipping away. That was more than likely due to the shock from the injury itself.

Errol came up behind her, rubbing his large hands up and down her forearms. "The bath will warm ye up. 'Tis been an eventful day. I was so frightened I was going to lose ye."

She turned and wrapped her arms around his waist, laying her head on his chest. Standing still, reveling in the heat of his body. The softness in his touch. Listening to the steady beat of his heart. It was all she needed and exactly the right thing she needed at this moment in time.

They said naught. Just stood there holding each other as if there were no other place that either of them could imagine they wanted to be.

A knock sounded and a maid called out from the other side of the door letting them ken the water for their bath had arrived.

Finally, they let go of each other and Errol opened the door to let the girls in. They curtsied to Errol and gave her warm smiles as they set to work emptying the buckets of steaming water into the large basin that was set in the corner, returning several times until it was full. Another maid brought a bundle of towels and heather soap.

After the maids had left, Errol turned to her. "As much as I would like this to be a luxurious, relaxing bath for the both of us, I think we need to wash the evidence of our last encounter off first."

He was referring to the dried blood encrusting their skin. And her wound that needed a good cleansing. The warrior, whose name she could not recall, cleansed it with ale to kill aught that could make it fester, but still, she was a dirty mess.

She agreed with him. The thought of sitting in water tinged red with blood and bits of things she didn't even want to think about was not appealing at all. At the wash basin, Moira wet a small square of cloth and gently washed Errol's face, cleaning off the blood splatter from his cheeks. His brow. His forehead. He had looked a sight when they appeared at the inn.

"Ye look like frightful," she said quietly, dabbing around his eyes. Eyes that watched her intently. "I can only imagine what the innkeeper was thinking when ye walked in."

"I am for certs that 'tis no' the first time he has seen a warrior come in and request accommodations."

"But I bet ye, none have been as fearsome as ye."

He chuckled, grasping her hand, his lips feathering over her fingers. "Ye are a boost to my ego, Lass."

That brought a smile to her lips.

She rinsed the cloth and brought it to Errol's bloodied knuckles, taking care as she cleaned the cuts. His fingers were already showing signs of bruising.

"Ye will be sore in the morn."

"Aye," he said when she finished. "The bastard and his family had been the cause of so much death and destruction that was assigned to the wrong people. Gavin and his men." He winced in pain. "They killed my brother. No' the Hart's. I am sorry, Moira. So verra sorry."

"Ye neednae apologize. Just as much as ye were blaming us, we were blaming ye. Our two families will need to go through a time of healing. We will need a full cleansing of the past. Mayhap a mighty gathering betwixt us all." She smiled. "I am happy that 'tis us that can start that healing."

She washed her hands, and gently rubbed her own swollen knuckles, shaking her head. "I dinnae ken how men use their punches so often. 'Tis painful."

Errol laughed, and brought his lips to her hand once again, kissing each knuckle gently. "Ye were verra brave. I was so proud."

Hands around her waist, he pulled her to where he sat, taking care not to touch her wounded area. She looked down at him. At his brown eyes that were filled with light and warmth, and something more that she couldn't quite identify.

"The water is getting cold. We dinnae want that to go to waste," he said quietly, wetting his lips.

That familiar aching began in her belly once again. A longing for something more.

"We wouldnae want that, would we?" She asked quietly.

He shook his head, his gaze catching hers as his fingers went to the ties of her dress.

Anticipation swirled around her like a dense fog rolling over the moors. Sucking her in. She let Errol undress her, his breath hitching when she stood naked in front of him. His brows creased when he looked at her recent stitches. When his eyes met hers again, she shook her head.

"Dinnae fret. Whilst the area is sore," she gently touched her fingertips to the area, "I have been hurt more falling out of a tree." She was being truthful. The area was tender to the touch, and she would have to take care not to open the stitches, but the pain was dull now that the shock of everything had worn off.

His hand lifted to caress her cheek. "Ye are perfectly beautiful, Moira Hart. I want to spend the rest of my days reveling in yer beauty."

Her cheeks heated, not from embarrassment, but from the compliment. She had never been looked upon in the way Errol was looking at her. As if he were drinking her in after a long thirst and he was parched. He led her over to the bath and helped her into the water.

She groaned as the heated water warmed her skin and relaxed her weary bones and muscles.

Standing beside the basin, Errol pulled his tunic over his head, revealing his broad chest, dusted with short, brown hair, his abdominal muscles reminded her of a ladder. She wanted to run her fingers along each line. Mayhap even her tongue. Och, the wicked thoughts that have started running rampant through her mind as he removed his boots and then pushed his trews down, revealing his manhood, standing tall, proud, stiff. Huge.

Her breath hitched as she caught her lower lip betwixt her teeth. He was the most beautiful thing she had ever seen.

And he was hers.

And she his.

Tonight, they would seal their union in the way as old as eternity, once again, bringing their families together as one. Their history coming full circle to completion.

With care, he climbed into the basin, settling behind her, his legs on either side of her, as she pushed forward to make room for him. She smiled at the thought of the innkeeper supplying them with an extra-large basin to accommodate them both. Had they been so obvious?

Errol wrapped an arm around her stomach, drawing her back gently so she lay flush against his front. She could feel his hardness at her back, and shivered.

He chuckled, his warm breath near her ear sent frissons running up and down her arms, making her skin pimple. Dipping the bar of soap in the water, he rubbed it into a clean cloth, creating a lather afore he ran it along her arm, lifting it and washing the underside. He repeated the motion on her other arm.

Urging her to sit up, he washed her back, then rinsed the water off afore drawing her back to him again.

Every inch of Moira's skin felt like it was aflame. Wherever Errol touched, goose pimples pebbled her skin.

He nuzzled her neck, his teeth lightly nipping at the sensitive column of her neck. Moving the washcloth over her breasts, her nipples peaked taut, and she arched her back at the sensation, ignoring the pull of her stitches, and moaned. Her skin felt alit. It was something she had never felt afore.

But then Errol dipped the cloth below the surface of the water and brought it to the apex of her thighs and she nearly jumped out of the basin with a squeak.

Grasping his wrist, she stilled Errol's hand. She took hold of the cloth and washed her nether region. What he was doing was exquisite, but she felt an odd feeling. Like a fireball knotting in her stomach and she wasn't sure how to handle it.

Turning, she looked at him over her shoulder. "My turn." Grabbing a clean cloth, she dunked it into the water and covered it with soap. The muscles of his broad shoulders bunched under her hands as she washed his shoulders, taking her time, letting the cloth run slowly over his skin. Then she moved to his chest where she noted the jump of his pectorals when she rubbed the cloth over them. Trailing the cloth down the center of his stomach, she could feel it ripple under her fingers.

Errol's eyes were intense, the pupils blown wide, as he watched her and when she moved to wash his still-hard manhood, he grasped her hand this time. "As much as I would love to have yer hands on me there, Lass. I willnae last."

She frowned, not fully understanding what he meant as he plucked the cloth from her hands and made quick work finishing to clean himself.

They rinsed off and then he urged her to stand, wrapping her in a towel afore stepping out himself and wrapping his own towel low on his hips. She caught her lower lip in her teeth at the vision in front of her. He was so fetching with a body that looked to be chiseled out of stone. Moving her closer to the fire, Errol rubbed her down with towel, taking care around her wound, patting the area tenderly.

"Ye are beautiful, Lass. I dinnae believe I have a seen a finer sight in all my life." In one swift move, he lifted her off her feet and carried her over to the bed, laying her gently on the soft throws.

As he dried himself off, her skin felt chilled, and nerves overcame her. Suddenly she felt anxious.

But when he joined her, covering her body with his, only heat consumed her.

Blistering, hot heat.

Capturing her mouth in a searing kiss, his fingers feathered down her sides, causing her to shiver. He smiled against her mouth. His fingers found the curls betwixt her legs, and he traced the seam of her slit, eliciting an "Oh!" from her.

Kissing his way down her body, his lips were warm against her neck, her collarbone. And absolute fire when they sucked a taut nipple into his mouth, his hand massaging her other breast, his fingers pinching and plucking at her nipple. The actions had her body lifting off the bed as the warmth in her stomach continued to grow.

Errol paused and looked up at her. "I love how yer body responds to me, Lass."

She wasn't sure what to say in response, but then his hand dropped to her mons again and he flicked his finger and she gasped.

His smile was huge as he held her gaze whilst he lowered himself, lower, and lower, until his mouth hovered over her apex. His warm breath fanning over her most private area, tickling the hairs there. He waggled his eyebrows as he pushed her knees upward, opening her up to him.

For a long moment, he stared, his eyes blazing. Gently blowing on her damp curls, she shuddered. And then his mouth was on her. Suckling, licking. Her hips lifted off the bed, and he placed his forearm on her stomach, keeping her still as he feasted on her body as if he were starving.

And she reveled in the feeling he awakened in her. Her body coming alive. An awakening she had never thought was possible. He sank a finger in to her folds and she couldn't help the moan that escaped her lips. In and out, he stroked her gently, then added another finger. Stroked more as her breath quickened, her body building higher and higher to something, but she didn't ken what.

Another finger sank into her as his mouth suckled on her. It was too much and not enough at the same time. She didn't ken what her body was doing. What it needed. She only kenned that she didn't want him to stop. She wanted more. The inferno kept building and building. The flames growing higher and higher as she thrashed her legs, her hands fisting Errol's shoulders.

She felt as if she were going to burst into thousands of pieces.

Suddenly, Errol was there, capturing her lips in his, she felt his hardness nudge her entrance. His mouth was at her ear. "'Twill hurt, but only for a moment. I promise."

Moira nodded. She didn't care. She only kenned she wanted more.

"Ready?"

She nodded and he pushed forward, breaching her maidenhead. A sharp pinch had her hitching her breath, as tears pricked her eyes.

Errol stilled, kissing her tears away. Then kissing her lips.

She felt stretched. Full.

But soon, the urge to move came. She didn't want him to be still. She wanted to feel him. All of him. Moving her hips in a small circle, she tested the feeling, and Errol remained unmoving as he watched her face, his own face strained, the veins in his forehead protruding and angry.

She rotated her hips again and sighed. Aye. That was what she wanted.

Nodding, she stroked Errol's cheeks and when he withdrew and filled her again, he caught her gasp on a kiss.

His hard body was the perfect match for her soft one. In and out he stroked, burying himself deep. His grunts and the look of pure bliss in his eyes, spurred her forward. She grasped his buttocks, squeezing them. Reveling at the feel of them. The tight muscles under her fingers bunched with each surge forward. His thrusts grew quicker, almost frantic.

Her breaths were coming so quickly, she could hardly catch them. Building. Building. That flaming inferno grew higher and higher. And then when Moira thought it couldn't possibly grow any larger, Errol reached between them and rubbed a spot that had her crying out his name as her whole body contracted. Her legs stiffened and then shuddered violently. Dots of light appeared in her vision as Errol quickened his pace, groaning her name until with a final deep thrust of his hips, her name tumbled from his lips as his whole body shook.

She stroked her hands up and down his back, smiling at how he shuddered with each movement.

Rolling onto his back, he brought her with him, settling her onto his chest, and kissed the top of her head.

"Are ye hurt?" He asked, his voice laced with concern.

She shook her head. "Nay. For the briefest of moments, but then 'twas all forgotten."

"And yer side? I should have taken more care."

She smiled, touched at his concern. "All is well. Ye were perfect."

"Sleep now." He drew the throw over them, and the sudden

exhaustion of the past few days caught up to her, making her eyelids heavy. No matter how much she wanted to fight it, she couldn't and soon succumbed to the pull of a blissful sleep.

◄───◆───►

CHAPTER TWENTY-THREE

RROL WOKE TO soft fingers drawing circles around his nipples and his cock roared to life. He grasped Moira's tiny fingers in his, stopping the sensuous torture.

"Should I no'?"

"'Tis no' that. How are ye feeling?"

She turned and rested her chin on his chest. "Sore. But in the best possible way." Her face grew serious. "When—when can we do that again?" She asked.

"Whene'er ye are ready, Lass." He brought her fingers to his lips. "Good morn, by the way."

"Good morn. So, now, then?"

"I thought ye said ye were sore."

She nudged him with her shoulder. "Aye, but I also said in the best possible way."

He smiled. "Come here." Pulling her over him, he lined up his hardness to her entrance and lifted his hips, hissing as he sank into her softness. "Sit up, Lass. Ride me."

Confusion darkened her eyes, until she understood what he was saying. And then she did, moving her hips rhythmically, and took his breath away. She rode him so sweetly as he reached out and tweaked her nipples, causing her to squeal. He lifted his hips and met her thrust for thrust. Felt his bollocks tighten. Christ. He couldn't last with this woman. He dropped his hand to her nestle of curls. Found the little bud of nerves and circled it with his thumb, applying pressure. She spasmed around him, squeezing him. Milking him. So impossibly tight.

Her legs stiffened on either side of him, and he flipped her onto her back, driving into her until he met his release. Her body drawing him in his release until he was truly spent.

He couldn't believe he almost missed this. If he hadn't listened to Moira. Or agreed to assist her. If he kept her away because she was a Hart. What a fool he would have been.

Slender arms wrapped around his neck. "I love ye, Errol."

He kissed the tip of her nose. "I love ye as well, Lass."

THEY SPENT THE ride back to MacLeod Keep learning more about each other. Moira spoke so openly he felt like he had kenned her for her whole life. He could see why she and Anna were so close.

As MacLeod Keep came into view, he straightened in his saddle. Robbie would have arrived already, giving his father the report of what had happened. Given him the treasure they had found. The letters. Information about MacPhail.

"Is something amiss?" Moira asked.

He softened his shoulders. He hadn't realized he was holding himself so rigid. "Nay. I am only thinking about our arrival."

Her smile faltered slightly. "It willnae be easy convincing our families of all that we have uncovered. Will it?"

He shook his head. "But we will."

They rode through the gates and into the courtyard, where Robbie waited, Errol's father beside him, arms crossed, a fierce look on his face.

Moira seemed to shrink in her saddle. "Dinna fash. All will be well. I promise ye."

They stopped their horses, and stable boys rushed forward to care for them.

He lifted Moira off her horse and set her on the ground, holding her steady so she didn't fall. "All is well, I promise," he whispered.

When their gazes met, she nodded, and when he clasped her hand to walk to his father, her eyes rounded.

His father stood stock still, eyes narrowed, arms still crossed. "In my study," he barked afore turning on his heel and heading into the keep, Robbie following him.

Anna rushed forward, wrapping her arms around Moira's neck in a tight hug. "Ye made it back!"

When Moira winced, his sister pulled away, brows drawn down in concern as she held Moira at arm's length to look her over. Moira's wound would heal just fine, and she kept insisting that she wasn't in any pain on their travel back home, but he got the feeling she was putting on a brave face so it didn't delay their arrival any longer.

Errol didn't hear the rest of Moira and Anna's conversation as he trailed his father to his study.

In the room, it was Errol, Robbie, his father, and his uncle.

"Sit." His father ordered and Errol did as he was told. But if his father told him that he would need to let Moira go, he was sorely mistaken.

"I have a messenger out to Laird Hart stating that his presence is required to discuss an important matter and to bring his family."

Errol's brows rose, but he said naught.

"Whilst I dinnae approve of how ye two went about what ye did, I must commend ye on yer findings."

"'Twas Moira mostly. She is smart. Strong. Brave."

His father held up his hand. "I can see that ye are enamored with her. Am I to assume that ye..." his father's words trailed off and Errol bit his lip.

But he wasn't ashamed of what had happened betwixt them. "She is to be my wife."

Laird MacLeod nodded. "I can see that. 'Twas evident the

moment ye rode through the gate."

"Does that mean ye approve?"

"Would it matter if I didnae?"

Errol grinned sheepishly. "Nay, but 'twould make things more difficult."

"There will be much to discuss with Laird Hart. We have years of strife to resolve. What ye have uncovered will help a lot with the healing that will require." He scratched his chin. "Now, ye defiling their eldest daughter, that will be a bigger hurdle."

"Da!" Errol snapped. "I didnae—"

His father raised a brow as if daring him to say that he hadn't made Moira his.

"Ye make it sound like she's some tavern wench. I love her."

His father's eyes rounded, and his uncle sucked in a breath.

But when he looked at Robbie, he had a kenning smile on his face as his head bobbed up and down. "Exactly as I had predicted. Ye were a lost pup the second ye laid eyes on the lass."

An hour later as Errol made his way through the keep to find Moira, he still couldn't believe what had transpired.

"Ye have my blessing."

His father said that. It nearly knocked Errol on his arse when the words left his father's lips.

He took the stairs two at a time, following the sound of excited giggles that could only be Anna and Moira's, along with their maids, since they'd all been reunited.

Knocking on the door, he heard them telling each other to be quiet. Anna opened the door, a wide grin splitting her face.

"Brother. To what do I owe the pleasure?" She asked innocently.

He tilted his head to the side. "Ye ken why I am here." He looked over her shoulder and met Moira's gaze and smiled.

She ran toward him, skirting around Anna and jumped into his arms, nuzzling into his neck.

"Careful, Lass," he warned. "Yer side." But Errol held her tight, spinning them around before setting her down on her feet.

He dug around in his pocket and closed his fingers around the gold band that he'd polished. It only made sense to continue the union of the MacLeod and the Hart with the rings that had started it all those years ago.

"Moira Hart. Ye have captured my heart, body, and soul. The thought of a day spent without ye is devastating. I fear I cannae live without ye. Will ye do me the biggest honor of becoming my wife?"

Moira's hands flew to her cheeks, swiping at the tears threatening to spill over.

Behind her, Anna, Fina, and Seema, were all jumping up and down, clapping their hands excitedly.

But Errol? He was stiff, worried, as he waited what seemed like an eternity for Moira to answer. But when she looked up at him with her big, blue, tear-filled eyes, a huge smile on her face as she nodded and jumped into his arms again, he kenned all would be right with the world.

"Aye, aye, aye!" She said, betwixt the kisses she peppered over his face afore finally settling on his lips.

"I've something for ye," he said as she hopped down, waiting patiently.

Withdrawing the ring, he smiled when recognition lit her face up. "'Tis their ring," she whispered in awe.

"Nay, 'tis ours now. 'Tis us that will rebirth the Hart and MacLeod union. We will continue the legacy they started all those years ago."

She sniffed, nodding as Errol slid the ring on her finger.

Their wedding would come later, planned with all the fanfare that Moira deserved. But until then, she was his, and he was hers.

EPILOGUE

Two Months Later

BELLS TOLLED FROM the chapel as Moira and Errol kissed for the first time as husband and wife. His strong arms wrapped around her waist as hers encircled his neck.

Witnessing their union was her family. All of them. Her parents. Brothers. Sisters.

Errol's family. Robbie. Anna. His uncle. His father.

Now they all smiled and clapped, but for a time it hadn't looked like the marriage would take place. It took a lot of convincing her parents that the MacLeod weren't bad people.

The fabricated facts of history had dictated their pasts, but they could change the future. Moira liked to think that they already had.

As they made their way to the Great Hall for a grand feast and celebration with music and dancing, Alpin approached Errol, clapping him on the back, congratulating him.

It was as if they were back in the times when they were younger. When being enemies wasn't their normal.

Thankfully, it wasn't anymore. But it took time. Her parents and Errol's father and uncle had pored over the clues and letters she and Errol had found, studying every detail. Every word. Until they all agreed—the MacPhail had enacted an elaborate scheme to cover up their crimes and put the Hart and MacLeod clans against each other and in the process took possession of the land that spanned betwixt theirs.

There was still a lot of healing that needed to be done. And it would come in time.

But the alignment of the two clans was a starting point to the healing that would inevitably come.

They did that. She and Errol.

Beside her, he gave her hand a squeeze.

They filled their bellies with delicious food. Danced until their feet ached, and just as they were ready to retire to Errol's bedchamber—and now hers—their parents took them aside.

"We have a wedding gift for ye, from the three of us." Lillias looked between her father and Errol's. At her urging, Errol's father spoke.

"The parcel of land betwixt ours. The original land that had been gifted to Thomas and Fiona." He cleared his throat. "We feel that 'tis only right that ye become the rightful owners of it now. 'Tis yers to build yer legacy upon."

"Did ye hear that, Errol?" Moira asked her new husband, who looked as dumbfounded as she felt.

"I did." He dropped into a bow. "Thank ye. I," he drew Moira near. "We will make ye proud."

"We've nay doubt. Congratulations to ye both." Her father said, then after shaking Errol's hand and placing a kiss on Moira's forehead, he clasped her mother's hand and drew her out into the dancing crowd of the clansfolk.

"Well, I will leave ye to, er, well, ye ken." Laird MacLeod hugged her. "Welcome to the family, Moira. Congratulations. I wish ye many years of happiness to come and lots of wee bairns." He spun and returned to the celebrations.

"I think we should get a start on the previously mentioned bairns. What say ye?" He grabbed her hand and practically pulled her up the stairs to his bedchamber.

And when he sank into her with a sigh, Moira sent a silent thank you up to Thomas and Fiona. Without them, none of this would be possible.

Errol worked his magic on her body. His fingers stroking all the right places. His tongue tasting her everywhere. And that familiar feeling that she'd grown to love was building, building, threatening to boil over and when it did, Errol was right there with her, grinding out her name through clenched teeth as they each met their release.

Later, when their breathing had calmed, and Moira drew lazy circles along Errol's abdomen, making the muscles jump and ripple in the way she found so fascinating, she thanked him.

"Thank ye for agreeing to help me. I ken ye didnae want to."

He grasped her hand, bringing it up to his lips and kissed her fingertips. "We set out to find treasure. And we did. I'm holding the most precious treasure in my arms. Lucky enough to spend the rest of my life gazing upon its brightness." He kissed her lips. "Ye are the best treasure one could hope to find, Moira Mac-Leod."

The End

About the Author

Award-winning author Brenna Ash is addicted to coffee, chocolate, and all things Scotland and BTS (the Korean band, not behind-the-scenes footage, though that can be fun, too!). She's a firm believer that one can never have too much purple or glitter. She loves rom-coms and always cries at the HEAs.

When she's not busy writing about Scottish Highlanders, Medieval Pirates, and Regency Rogues, she spends her time reading with her favorite music playing in the background, binge-watching Outlander, Bridgerton, and K-dramas, park-hopping with her daughter, spoiling her cats, Lilly and Mochi, or watching BTS content online. Brenna lives with her husband on the Space Coast in sunny Florida.

Website – www.brennaash.com
Amazon – amazon.com/stores/author/B01H46ZA02
Facebook – BrennaAshAuthor
Instagram – brennaashauthor
BookBub – bookbub.com/profile/brenna-ash

www.ingramcontent.com/pod-product-compliance
Lightning Source LLC
Chambersburg PA
CBHW060411310726
48976CB00003B/1012